Glub . . . Glub . . . Glub.

Tad is hoping for a little fun in the sun this summer. So why is he so bummed when his parents decide to go to the super-cool water resort Club Lagoona? Because Tad's afraid of water. He hates everything about it. And he can't swim.

But that's not the only reason Tad should be afraid. At Club Lagoona there's something living under the surface of the Atlantis Pool.

Something green.

Something slimy.

Something hungry!

Also from R.L. Stine

The Beast®
The Beast® 2

Available from MINSTREL Books

THE CREATURE
FROM CLUB LAGOONA

A Parachute Press Book

A
MINSTREL®
BOOK

Published by POCKET BOOKS
New York   London   Toronto   Sydney   Tokyo   Singapore

This book is a work of fiction. Names, characters, places and incidents are products of the author's imagination or are used fictitiously. Any resemblance to actual events or locales or persons, living or dead, is entirely coincidental.

A MINISTREL PAPERBACK *Original*

A Ministrel Paperback published by
POCKET BOOKS, a division of Simon & Schuster Inc.
1230 Avenue of the Americas, New York, NY 10020

Copyright © 1997 by Parachute Press, Inc.

THE CREATURE FROM CLUB LAGOONA WRITTEN BY
GLORIA HATRICK

All rights reserved, including the right to reproduce
this book or portions thereof in any form whatsoever.
For information address Pocket Books, 1230 Avenue
of the Americas, New York, NY 10020

ISBN: 0-671-00850-1

First Minstrel Books paperback printing June 1997

10   9   8   7   6   5   4   3   2   1

FEAR STREET is a registered trademark of Parachute Press, Inc.

A MINISTREL BOOK and colophon are registered trademarks of
Simon & Schuster Inc.

Cover art by Broeck Steadman

Printed in the U.S.A.

R·L·STINE'S
GHOSTS of FEAR STREET ®

THE CREATURE
FROM CLUB LAGOONA

I

"'**C**lub Lagoona,'" Mom read from the booklet. She had to practically shout to be heard over the small plane's engines. "'The water adventure of a lifetime!'" She grinned at me.

I pointed to my ear and shook my head. Maybe if I pretended I couldn't hear her, she'd give up.

But she continued reading. "'Relax in Club Lagoona's fabulous saltwater Atlantis Swimming Pool. You'll think you're in the ocean.'" She stopped and squeezed my arm. "It's the biggest pool in the world, Tad! Sounds great, huh?"

I tried to smile. "Can't wait." I put my copy of *Jaws* down on my lap. The plane was really small, and we were the only passengers, so I glanced out the round airplane window.

Maybe I shouldn't have. Below me was endless ocean. Probably crawling with sharks.

"I'm going to snorkel! And learn to scuba dive!" Polly, my younger sister, shouted from across the aisle. She's nine and loves to swim.

"Listen to this," Dad chimed in. He had a copy of the booklet too. "They've got a glass-bottomed boat, a Log Flume of Doom, and something called the Creature Water Slide!"

"Great!" Polly shouted. She would have bounced out of her seat if she weren't strapped in.

"How about you, Tad?" Dad flashed the booklet at me. "You ready for the Log Flume of Doom?"

"Count me in," I replied. I gave him two thumbs-up.

I picked up my book again and flipped nervously through the pages. How could I tell them the truth? I'd kept my secret for twelve years. I covered it up so well that no one guessed.

They probably wouldn't have believed the truth anyway. They would never have imagined that I, Tad Hawkins, captain of the Shadyside Middle School soccer team, king of slam dunks, all-around jock, was actually scared to death of—

"Let's get wet!" Polly squealed, interrupting my thoughts. "That's Club Lagoona's motto. Cool!"

I slammed my book shut.

Water. Water scares me to death.

2

I hate the way water gets in my nose and eyes. I hate the way my wet hair sticks to my face and neck. And I particularly hate not knowing what's *under* the water. I guess I hate *everything* about water.

All these years I avoided swimming lessons by being too busy with soccer and basketball.

But at Club Lagoona, there would be no escape!

"Ready to *get wet,* Tad?" Polly shrieked at me. She kicked her feet against her seat.

I ignored her.

"Don't be such a wet blanket, Tad," Polly teased. "Get it? *Wet* blanket?"

I shot her a nasty look. She tugged her baseball cap low over her dark hair. But I could still see her green eyes laughing at me.

Polly and I look alike. "Like two peas in a pod," Mom always says. But, boy, are we different. Especially when it comes to water.

"Can you keep it down, Polly?" I complained. "I'm trying to read."

"How can you read now?" Polly demanded. "We're going to Club Lagoona! All the kids in Shadyside are totally jealous. Club Lagoona looked awesome in the TV commercials! And even better in the booklet!" She waved a brochure at me. Then she opened it up to read from it.

"Everything in Club Lagoona has to do with water," Polly reported. "The rooms are decorated in blue

3

and green. There's an underwater restaurant. And there's even a video arcade with the new, advanced Underwater Terror 2 game!"

"Great," I grumbled.

It all sounded like torture to me.

I've been scared of water for as long as I can remember. I still think about the time I lost my tooth in the bathtub. It was sucked right down the drain.

I shuddered, trying to shake off the image of that vanishing tooth. Swirling and swirling down that dark hole. I lowered my eyes to my book again. The shark in the book circled a kid on a raft. It moved closer and closer. It opened its mouth. It—

"Got you!" my sister yelled, reaching across Mom and jabbing me with her snorkel.

My head nearly hit the roof of the plane. "Quit it!" I shouted back.

"Stop arguing, kids," Mom ordered.

"Look," Dad called. "We're here!"

I closed my book and gazed out the window. Lagoona Island was a small private island off the Carolina coast. The only thing on it was Club Lagoona.

Oh, man! Not only was the island surrounded by all that ocean, there was water all over the island!

The tallest fountain I'd ever seen sprayed straight up into the air. A gigantic pool of water shimmered

4

nearby. People on Jet Skis zoomed around a wide moat circling the hotel.

A helicopter hovered nearby. I could see someone dropping boxes marked SUPPLIES out of the helicopter to the moat-surrounded resort. That's weird, I thought. Why don't they just carry the stuff there?

I flopped back against my seat and shut my eyes. I had a feeling this was going to be the most awful vacation in the history of the world.

"That must be the landing strip," Mom pointed out, leaning over my shoulder.

Dad and Polly looked out their side of the plane. "I think I can see the Log Flume of Doom!" Polly cried.

"Come on, everybody. We'll be landing in a minute. Grab your stuff," Dad commanded.

I shoved my book into my backpack and within minutes we all piled off the plane. We gathered at the colorful entrance sign to Club Lagoona. I squinted in the bright sunlight and gazed across the broad moat. Exotic smells filled my nostrils.

"It looks like a fairy-tale kingdom by the sea!" Polly whispered.

"A tropical paradise!" Mom agreed.

"A fantasy island!" Dad added.

My worst nightmare, I thought.

"Welcome to Club Lagoona!" a voice boomed over a

loudspeaker. "Get set for the water adventure of a lifetime!"

The tall bushes made it hard to see what was on the other side of the moat. But I knew all the same— *water*. And lots of it!

Polly stood up on tiptoe. "I see water towers and slides!"

"Just look at those palm trees!" Mom added.

"Listen!" Dad commanded.

As we stood in silence, I could hear the sound of water rushing and people shouting and laughing.

"Let's go in!" Polly urged.

"How are we supposed to get to the hotel?" I demanded. "The whole place is surrounded by water!"

We all stared at the moat. It stood between us and the resort.

"Do we get to swim across?" Polly exclaimed, all excited.

Mom laughed and shook her head. "Sorry, Polly. There's a sign pointing to a bridge."

I shouldered my backpack and trudged slowly behind the others.

Ahead of us was a rickety rope bridge. The kind you see in Indiana Jones movies. The kind that always gives way when someone's halfway across. So *that's* why they can't carry supplies to the resort, I realized.

I stopped walking. "Uh, is that thing safe?" I asked.

"It must be safe," Mom replied. "There's no other way to get into Club Lagoona."

"Sure," Dad added. "It's perfectly safe. Look." He took a few steps onto the bridge. He jumped up and down. The bridge shook but didn't break.

I watched the three of them make their way across. The bridge wobbled, but it looked as if it would hold me. I didn't like the way the bridge seemed to dip in the middle though. It practically touched the water.

That made me nervous.

I stepped onto the bridge. It jiggled a little, but I took a deep breath, gripped both handrails, and kept going.

I stared straight ahead. One foot in front of the other. That's it, I told myself. You're doing fine.

"Hurry up, Tad," Polly shouted from the other side. "We're missing all the fun!"

That's when I made a mistake. I looked down.

Water. On both sides of me. And there I was, stuck right in the middle of it.

I swallowed hard. The bridge shook more violently. Then I realized my trembling knees were making it vibrate.

Just keep your eyes straight ahead, I ordered myself. Stay focused on Polly, Mom, and Dad. And keep walking. That's the only way off the bridge—without getting wet!

I approached the middle of the bridge. My heart

pounded harder. The bridge sank even farther than I thought, dipping just a little into the moat.

Water sloshed over my feet, soaking my sneakers. I gripped the handrails harder.

I trudged on, teeth clenched, feeling the water swirl around my ankles.

Then something caught my attention, just outside my view. What was it? I turned quickly to face it.

Something black and triangular cut smoothly through the water.

Is that a *fin?* I wondered. I thought of the horrible shark in my book. The black triangle disappeared behind me.

Panic made my whole body shudder. I tried to calm down.

There wouldn't be a shark in the moat, I reassured myself. It would be too dangerous for the people at the resort. It had to be my imagination.

But then I thought about *Jaws.* Nobody believed there was a shark there either. Not at first.

I took five deep breaths to calm down. Then I started walking again. The other side of the moat grew closer. I was nearly there. I was going to make it across.

"Tad! Look out!" Polly screamed.

I heard a splash. Something behind me broke the surface of the water. Waves washed over my feet.

The rickety bridge shook and swayed.

I clung to the sides, desperately trying not to fall.

I glanced over my shoulder.

The biggest shark I had ever seen rose up out of the water. Its massive jaws opened, revealing a mouthful of deadly teeth.

Then it lunged for me!

2

~~~

"**N**ooooooooo!" I shrieked.

Rows of razor-sharp teeth flashed in the sunlight. I let go of the handrails and covered my head. I backed up against one of the rope rails, trying to escape the shark. I held my breath, waiting for the sharp teeth to chomp down on me.

Nothing happened.

Did the shark sink back underwater? Did I frighten it with my scream? Or was it under the bridge, about to attack from the other side?

I peeked between my fingers.

The shark waited right in front of me now. Huge. Menacing. Awesome.

And only inches from my face. It opened and shut

its massive jaws. I froze. Was I going to be a shark snack?

The jaws opened again.

"Welcome to Club Lagoona!" a tinny voice said.

Huh? A talking shark? I leaned forward. I could see a tiny speaker in the shark's throat!

"It's time to *get wet!*" the shark added. A stream of water shot from its mouth. It squirted me in the face.

Then the shark sank under the water again.

It's a robot fish! I realized. Of course! Like the ones they use in movies.

I plastered a big smile on my face and tried to look casual. As if I hadn't been faked out by a mechanical fish. I could hear Polly laughing hysterically as I dried my face on my T-shirt.

"Get wet!" she shouted. She laughed so hard, she doubled over.

I shot her my nastiest look.

"Come on, Tad," Dad called. "Quit clowning around. Let's get checked in."

Checking in was the last thing I wanted to do. I was ready to turn around and head home.

I joined my family at the entrance to the club. The building looked like a gigantic whale head. To get in, we had to walk into the whale's wide-open mouth.

Cute.

Inside the whale's mouth was the lobby of Club Lagoona. I had to admit, it was pretty amazing. Huge banana trees and coconut trees grew right up to the high glass roof. Red and blue parrots flew around free. Tiny green chameleons scampered among tropical plants.

The reception desk stood in the center of the room. Polly, Mom, and Dad clustered at the desk. They were firing hundreds of questions at the receptionist.

"Sign me up for scuba lessons and a trip on the glass-bottomed boat!" Polly requested.

"Great!" the receptionist replied cheerfully. "And what about water-skiing?"

"Sure!" Dad agreed. "Put me down for that!"

I flopped into a chair beside the desk. It was shaped like an open clamshell. I wished it would just close up, and I could spend the rest of the vacation hiding inside. *Not* getting wet.

"Tad?" Dad turned and glanced at me. "You want us to sign you up for all this great stuff?"

"Sure," I mumbled. "Put me down for everything." Then I had an idea. "Hey, do you have soccer or basketball here?" I asked hopefully.

"Sure do!" the receptionist bubbled.

My hopes rose. I darted over to the desk, ready to sign up. Hooray! I would be able to avoid swimming after all.

"Want me to put you down for Aqua Goals and Wet Hoops?" she asked.

"Aqua Goals and Wet Hoops?" I repeated uncertainly.

She laughed. "They're the Club Lagoona version of soccer and basketball. We play in the pool! Even better than boring land games, because this way we can all—" She paused and gazed at my family.

"Get wet!" they shouted in unison.

Get me out of this place, I thought. My entire family is turning into a bunch of aqua-nuts.

The receptionist lined us up for a photo. As soon as she snapped the camera, my family unfroze and began firing questions at her again. "I'm sure we have activities for all of you," I heard her say as I wandered off.

I explored the reception area. Maybe I would find *something* that didn't involve water. The lobby floor was blue and white marble. Everything else—the walls, the decorations, even the Club Lagoona uniforms—was aqua. I felt as if I were already in the water just being there.

Scattered around the walls were large color photographs of the attractions at the club. I found a picture of the Log Flume of Doom. It was really high. Really *really* high! Everyone in the picture looked as if they were screaming as they shot down the flume! Right into the deep pool below. Definitely one ride to avoid.

Another picture was of the Creature Water Slide. It showed people riding tubes down an amazingly tall slide. The slide was shaped like a giant Loch Ness monster. Another no-no for me.

Then I came to an aerial shot of the whole resort. It

13

was huge. No doubt about it—I was definitely stuck on an island. Completely surrounded by water. And I could see that the moat circled the entire resort. No escape—except for the rickety rope bridge.

I wandered through a doorway into a long hall. More photos lined the walls. I stared at them as I continued walking.

"Oops! Excuse me," I said as I collided with someone else. I turned to see who I bumped into. A very short man wearing a bright green jump suit stood in front of me. My nose wrinkled. I could smell chlorine. I figured that must be what he carried in his bucket.

"It's okay," he said. He had bushy gray hair and nearly black eyes. He stared at me a minute. Then he peered around nervously. "I saw you on the rope bridge just now," he whispered.

Oh, great. I sighed. People had seen the dorky way I acted on the bridge. I felt my face flush. "Pretty silly, huh?" I smiled weakly. "Being scared by a mechanical fish."

The man glanced around again. He stepped closer to me. "You're not silly at all," he assured me. He seemed nervous, as if he didn't want anyone to overhear him. "This place is dangerous. Take my advice—watch out for the deep end!"

"Huh?" What deep end? What was this guy talking about? I wondered.

But before I could ask, the little man turned and hurried away. "Wait!" I called after him.

Mom, Dad, and Polly rushed up to me. The little man disappeared around a corner.

"All set, Tad," Dad declared. "We signed you up for just about everything."

I nodded. But I wasn't really listening. Instead, I thought about the little man's warning. Could things really be dangerous around here?

"That nice young woman at the desk took care of our luggage, so let's check out the grounds," Mom suggested. "I want to see the restaurant and the gym."

"I want to see *everything!*" Polly cheered.

I trailed along behind them, but I kept thinking about the little man with the chlorine bucket. Who was he? Why did he look so nervous? Why should I watch out for the deep end? The deep end of *what?*

I tried to imagine what there was to be afraid of. After all, the scary shark turned out to be mechanical. And Club Lagoona was a resort. A place for people to have fun.

But something about the man bothered me. The way he whispered and kept glancing around. Why was he being so careful—as if he were letting me in on some sort of secret?

"Tad, you're not keeping up," Mom called. "Don't you want to explore with us?"

I'd seen more than enough already. "I think I'll find my room and unpack." My family stared at me as if I were nuts. I guess they couldn't imagine why anyone would want to be in a hotel room when they could be out *getting wet*.

"My sneakers are soaked and my shirt's wet from being sprayed by the shark," I explained. "I figured I'd change my clothes."

"That's probably a good idea," Mom said. "We'll find one another later." She handed me a small map of the resort. Our rooms were marked with X's. Then they rushed away.

I located my room on the map. Polly and I were sharing a suite separate from Mom and Dad's. Well, at least there was *one* cool thing about staying at Club Lagoona—our own hotel room.

The rooms were situated along the moat. Ours were directly across the island from the reception area. To get there, I'd have to use the main boardwalk. Signs pointed out different attractions along the way. I heard the sound of splashing and laughter all around me as I crossed the island.

Soon I came to the middle of the resort and recognized the enormous fountain we'd seen from the plane. Circled around the fountain were the main attractions: the Log Flume of Doom, the Creature Water Slide, and the huge pool Mom read about— the Atlantis Swimming Pool. Sand surrounded everything—just like at the beach.

Between the three main attractions were restaurants, stores, and games arcades. I figured I could explore on my way back, so I hurried on to the suite.

I found the room without any trouble. Once inside, I stepped out of my soggy sneakers. I yanked off my wet T-shirt and tossed it on the bed. Since it was really warm, and since most of the people I saw on the way to the room wore bathing suits, I didn't bother putting a new shirt on. Wearing just my shorts, I headed back out to find my family.

I headed over to the Log Flume of Doom. People screamed as they hurtled down a river in a log-shaped boat. Everyone made a huge splash at the bottom and got soaked. Kids and their parents screamed and laughed, all having fun.

At the Creature Water Slide a kid zoomed down backward, riding a tube shaped like a seahorse. He grinned from ear to ear.

If only I weren't afraid of the water, I thought, I could be having fun like everyone else.

I remembered that little man telling me the place was dangerous. He said I wasn't silly to be scared. But I *felt* silly. Really silly. In fact, I felt like a big weenie.

I kicked at some sand and nearly tripped on the edge of a pool. I shaded my eyes and tried to see to the other side. I couldn't, it was so big. I figured it was about the size of two football fields.

The Atlantis pool.

I shuddered and took a quick step back.

Crowds of laughing people splashed and played nearby. I watched as boys and girls dunked each other and parents taught little kids to swim. Kids much smaller than me were having a great time in the shallow end. And here I was, terrified just by being this close to the pool.

My head whipped around at the sound of a loud crack. A teenage boy was jumping up and down on a high diving board. I shaded my eyes again and read the sign posted beside the board. "Deep end," I murmured. There were no other people near him.

I watched with weak knees as the guy jumped higher and higher on the end of the board. His green and yellow bathing suit practically glowed in the bright sunlight.

He jumped again, bouncing higher than ever. This time he soared off the end of the board. I held my breath as he somersaulted once, twice, then plunged straight into the deep end. He broke the surface of the water cleanly, sharp as a knife.

Then he disappeared.

I waited anxiously for him to come up.

It seemed to take forever. I slowly walked toward the diving board, never taking my eyes off the spot where he'd disappeared.

A loud whirring sound startled me. At first I couldn't tell where it was coming from. Then I realized the sound came from the deep end of the pool—where the diver had disappeared!

I dashed closer to the side. How could he stay down for so long? Did he hit his head on the bottom or something? And the whirring—was it some kind of machinery or equipment? Did the diver get caught in it somehow?

The whirring noise suddenly stopped. Immediately, hundreds of bubbles rose to the surface of the water.

Those bubbles must have been the diver's, I realized. He must have stopped holding his breath!

I shaded my eyes and hoped for a sign of the bright yellow and green bathing suit. All I could see was the deep aqua of the pool.

The bubbles stopped rising to the surface of the water.

And still no diver!

Sweat beaded across my forehead. My legs and hands trembled.

Where was he?

The deep end of the Atlantis pool became calm and quiet.

I shivered, my stomach curdling.

Oh, no, I thought.

The diver's gone!

3

"Help!" I screamed. "Someone's drowning!"

I raced up and down the edge of the pool. "Lifeguard!" I screamed. "Where's a lifeguard?"

My eyes darted around the area. There were several lifeguard chairs lining the side of the pool. They were all empty.

I searched for something to throw into the water. An inner tube. A rope, even. But I couldn't find anything. And what good would it do anyway? The diver hadn't even surfaced yet.

But I had to do *something*.

If only I knew how to swim! I stood at the edge, gazing at the water. Wishing I could dive in and save him.

But there was no way. Even if I were brave enough to jump in, I'd just drown myself.

"Help!" I bellowed again. I've never shouted so loud in my entire life.

Someone raced toward me from the shallow end. "I'm a lifeguard," he called. "What's wrong?"

"Someone's drowning!" I cried. "He dove off the board into the deep end!" I pointed to where I'd seen the bubbles. "He never came up!"

The lifeguard whipped his whistle and sunglasses off. He dove straight in and swam to where I pointed. "Here?" he demanded, turning back toward me.

"Yes! Hurry!" I shouted.

The lifeguard tucked and disappeared underwater.

I raced back and forth along the side. I didn't know what else to do. I couldn't stop my hands from shaking.

It seemed to take forever before the lifeguard surfaced.

He swam quickly to the side and hauled himself out. "I searched all around," he explained between breaths. "There's no one down there."

"There has to be!" I protested. "I watched him dive in just a few minutes ago! He never came back up!"

The lifeguard smiled. "He probably swam underwater to the shallow end and climbed out. Or maybe he got out when you were looking for help. You just didn't see him."

I shook my head. I knew he hadn't gotten out at all. All that came up were those bubbles.

The lifeguard patted my arm. "Don't worry. I'm sure the guy's fine. Honest."

I wanted to believe him. "Maybe you're right," I agreed reluctantly.

"Tad! Are you okay?" Mom called. She and Dad rushed over to us.

"We were having a snack at the Sand Bar," Dad huffed. "We heard you shouting. What's wrong?"

"It was just a mistake," the lifeguard explained. "Your son thought he saw someone in trouble. But it's okay. No one has drowned."

"Thanks for your help," Dad told the lifeguard. "Sorry for the false alarm."

"No problem. That's my job," the lifeguard replied, and jogged off.

"Nice to know they're on their toes," Dad said. "Well, I think I'm ready for a swim. How about you two?"

"Good idea," Mom agreed. "Let's get Polly and go put on our suits."

I didn't say a word. There was no way I was putting even my big toe in that water. Not after that diver disappeared in the deep end.

I suddenly remembered the strange little man. Didn't he tell me to watch out for the deep end?

Could the vanishing diver have something to do with his weird warning?

I shook my head. Too many thoughts were spinning around in there! Then I heard a small splash from the pool behind me.

Something grabbed me by the ankle.

Something cold and wet.

It pulled me closer to the edge of the pool!

"AAAAGGHHH!" I shrieked, shaking my leg loose. I glared down into the pool.

A big, wet, grinning face gazed back.

"Hey, it's okay," the guy said, hauling himself out of the pool. He wore a wet-suit top and dark shorts. The words "Swimming Instructor" were embroidered on the top. Underneath that it said "Barracuda."

"Didn't mean to scare you there, fella." He laughed and patted my back. "Just thought you might want to *get wet!*"

I chuckled hesitantly. "Uh—sure. Thanks," I told the guy.

He stuck out his hand. I shook it. "The name's Barry."

"I'm Tad," I told him. Barry's hand was soaking wet. I wiped the water off my hand on my shorts.

He pointed to the "Barracuda" embroidered on his wet-suit top. "Barry's short for Barracuda, my Club Lagoona name. Everyone who visits here gets a Club Lagoona name."

"Cool!" Polly's voice came from behind me. She darted over to join us. "My real name's Polly, so what's my Club Lagoona name?"

Barry smiled at her. "That's easy. You'll be Pollywog."

"Pollywog," she repeated. "I like it. My mom's name is Catherine. Bet you can't think of a special name for her."

Barry gazed at Mom. "Catherine. Catherine," he murmured. "How about Catfish?"

Mom laughed. "Well, I don't have whiskers, but I like cats. Okay, I'll be Catfish."

"Dad is Raymond. Ray for short," Polly explained. "I know a good one for him."

"Stingray!" Polly and Barry shouted together.

Ugh! How dorky! I thought I was going to puke.

But Dad seemed pleased with his name.

"Tad's next!" Polly shouted. "What's his Club Lagoona name?"

I knew they'd get to me.

Barry rubbed his chin and looked me up and down. His eyes twinkled.

I braced myself for the worst. I had a good idea of what name they'd come up with.

"Tad can be—Tadpole!" Barry exclaimed.

"Just what I was thinking!" Polly giggled.

Yup. Tadpole. Exactly what I figured they'd call me. Talk about corny. Maybe Polly didn't mind being named for a fat baby frog, but I did!

"Say, have you guys heard about the big race?" Barry asked.

Race? I could feel my stomach tighten.

We all shook our heads. I shook mine hardest.

"It's kind of a Club Lagoona initiation," Barry explained. "We call it Sink or Swim." He punched my arm lightly. "It's where we separate the rocks from the jocks."

"Huh?" I asked.

"Rocks and jocks," he repeated. "The rocks sink. The jocks swim. But here at Club Lagoona, everyone takes lessons. We feel there's always room for improvement, whether you're a rock or a jock. Right, Tad?"

"Yeah, sure," I agreed weakly.

"Sounds like fun," Dad told Barry. "Tad here is sure to be one of the jocks. He's his soccer team captain, you know."

Sure. I'm a jock. But only on land, Dad, I corrected him silently.

"Tad," Mom said. "Why don't you stay here with Barry while Dad, Polly, and I change into our bathing suits."

"Great!" Barry cried.

My parents and Polly headed for our rooms. Barry grabbed my shoulder and steered me over to the edge of the pool. "Come on, jock! *Let's get wet!*"

My brain went numb with panic. Barry moved me

closer and closer to the edge of the pool. There was no way out of this!

I glanced around. There were hundreds of people in the pool. Hundreds of people who would see that *I couldn't swim!* Well, at least when I started to drown, there would be enough people around to save me.

I bent over and gazed down into the aqua water. The image of the disappearing diver floated before me. What would happen to *me* down there in all that water?

And what about the little man's warning about the place being dangerous?

My heart beat faster. I started to tremble.

Give up the act, Tad, I ordered myself. Confess you can't swim. Or it's all over.

I had to get out of there. I straightened up, ready to bolt.

Then a hard shove came from behind! Right in the middle of my back!

I grabbed armfuls of air. My legs kicked.

I hit the water in a giant belly flop.

The skin on my face and stomach burned from the slap of the water.

I sank. Like a rock. Deep into the water.

I shut my eyes and held my breath.

Everything I hate about the water started happening. Water seeped into my ears. It shot straight up my nose.

I panicked and opened my eyes. The saltwater burned so much, I could barely see. My mouth opened and water rushed down my throat, choking me.

I flailed around, trying to touch the bottom with my feet. But I couldn't! The water was too deep. I was in over my head!

I'm going to drown! I thought, wild with panic.

I struggled to the top for air. When I got there, I could see Barry standing calmly on the side. He smiled down at me, watching. Waiting for me to prove what a jock I was.

I knew I'd have to fake it. And maybe I wouldn't drown.

Maybe.

I gulped a big breath of air. I tried to move my arms and legs the way I'd seen swimmers do.

I stretched my arms out in front of me and brought them around. They pulled me forward a little.

Then I kicked my legs out behind me kind of like a frog. But instead of moving forward, I somehow went backward!

This wasn't working at all.

I'm in big trouble! I thought.

I gasped for breath again. I felt myself sinking.

My shoulders dipped below the surface. I tilted my face to keep it out of the water.

I opened my mouth to scream.

And swallowed what seemed like a gallon of water.

I sputtered furiously as I plunged to the bottom of the pool.

Oh, no! I thought. I'm drowning!

4

I fought with every muscle against sinking. But I was so tired from struggling.

My lungs were ready to burst. My arms and legs felt heavy. I could barely move them through the water. I tried to stroke. I tried to kick. But I didn't seem to move any closer to the surface.

Then I heard the noise. That same strange whirring I'd noticed before. The whirring that I heard when the diver vanished. It came from somewhere in the pool.

My eyes adjusted to the saltwater. I caught a glimpse of something large and green in the pool with me.

It was long and thick. Maybe I could grab it and save myself! I tried to paddle toward it.

Luckily it was heading my way!

I tried to focus my eyes on it. What could it be? A log? No, it wiggled too much.

The strange green thing moved closer. Suddenly it lashed out! It wrapped around my arm.

That's when I realized what it was.

A tentacle.

An enormous sea creature had me in its slimy, powerful grasp!

My arms and legs jerked into action. I had no control over them. My hands reached out as if I were clutching the water ahead of me. My legs shot out behind me and kicked like crazy.

I couldn't worry about drowning. My only thought was to get away. To get out of that pool!

I plowed through the water, my heart pounding. The tentacle slid off my arm.

My body kicked into high gear now. The water split in front of me.

I broke through the surface so fast, I rose out of the water. I sucked in giant gulps of air. I caught a glimpse of the side of the pool.

Barry still stood there, watching me.

I didn't waste any time. I flung myself through the water.

A minute later my knuckles scraped against cement. I grabbed the side and locked on. In one smooth motion I pulled my body right out of the pool.

I lurched onto the sand, gasping for breath.

Barry stood over me. "Your form needs some major work, Tadpole. But, boy, was that fast!" he said.

My heart pounded. I struggled to catch my breath. I had to tell Barry. I swam like that only because I had to escape a monster!

I panted and wheezed.

Finally, I stood up. "Barry." I coughed. "Listen, I have to tell you. There's something weird in that pool. Some kind of—monster!"

Barry stared at me. Grinning.

"I know this sounds crazy," I continued, "but I saw a diver disappear in the deep end. He went down and never came back up. I heard this weird whirring noise. And that's not all." My words came faster and faster. "Something came up from the deep end just now. It was big and green. It looked like a tentacle. It reached out and grabbed my arm!"

Barry smiled. "Big and green, huh?" he asked.

"Yes!" I nodded.

"And kind of long and squiggly?" he continued. I nodded again.

"Tad, what grabbed you wasn't a monster. It was a piece of seaweed." Barry laughed.

"Seaweed?" I demanded. "No way. What would seaweed be doing in a pool?"

"Club Lagoona promises to give you the water adventure of a lifetime. Right?" Barry asked.

"Yeah . . ." I said uncertainly.

"So we try to make everything as realistic as possible. Our saltwater Atlantis pool actually has seaweed growing from the bottom. Neat, huh?" Barry punched my arm.

I thought about the thing that grabbed me. It was big and green and kind of slimy. Maybe it was seaweed.

Maybe.

"Lighten up, Tad!" Barry shook his head at me. "That's what Club Lagoona is all about. Having fun, relaxing, and *getting wet!*" He dipped his foot in the pool and splashed me.

"Don't forget, Tad, your Sink or Swim trial is first thing tomorrow morning. That's where we separate the rocks from the jocks! The 'sinkers' from the 'swimmers.' Your performance in that race will determine which swimming class you'll be in," Barry explained. "From what I saw just now, I doubt you'll be swimming with the Sharks, but—"

"The *Sharks?*" I interrupted, my eyes wide.

"The advanced swimming class," Barry explained. "They're called the Sharks! But remember, no matter how good—or bad—you are, Club Lagoona will make you a better swimmer. So on your last day we have another Sink or Swim relay. We like to see how much everyone has improved. Cool, huh?"

"Yeah." I gulped. "Cool."

Barry jogged off. I gazed into the pool. Okay. I

32

might be wrong about the monster. But one thing I knew for sure.

Where water was concerned, I was no jock. I was definitely a rock!

And I was about to sink at the Sink or Swim!

5

My eyes popped open the next morning. A pair of eyes stared back at me.

Fish eyes.

I sat straight up in bed. I glanced around the room. Of course. My first full day at Club Lagoona.

I sighed when I saw the fish-shaped light fixture that hung from the ceiling in my room.

I gazed at the fish painted on the walls. The bedspread covered with seashells. The fishing net hanging from the ceiling. Even my pillow was shaped like a clam.

I shook my head. "There's definitely something fishy about this room," I joked. I cracked myself up.

"So you're finally awake," Polly called from the bathroom we shared. "Mom and Dad will be here any minute. We're heading over to the Atlantis pool together."

I flopped back down on the bed. The Atlantis pool. The Sink or Swim trial with Barry. It was this morning!

I had to find a way out of this. And it was going to take some pretty fast thinking!

Polly bounced into my room. She wore a black and bright purple bathing suit. "Mom unpacked your stuff," she informed me. "Your new bathing suit is in the top drawer. And hurry up!" She yanked the covers off me.

"Okay. Okay," I grumbled. I stumbled over to the dresser and yanked open the top drawer.

Oh, man.

I reached in and pulled out the most hideous bathing suit I had ever seen.

I twirled the trunks between my fingers. Green volcanoes spewed bright orange lava. In between the volcanoes were nauseating purple and red flowers.

Well, at least I would never have to wear the awful thing. Since there was no way I was getting into the pool! I buried the suit under a pile of T-shirts.

No bathing suit, no Sink or Swim.

Dad knocked and popped his head into the room. "You kids ready?" he asked. He stepped inside. Mom followed behind him.

"It's time to *get wet!*" they cheered together.

35

I cringed. I had to get out of this. I couldn't let them discover my secret.

"I—uh—I can't find my bathing suit," I stammered.

"No problem, Tad," Mom reassured me. "We just stopped at the Wet Set Boutique, and I couldn't resist these."

She handed me a pair of swimming trunks. These were even worse than the volcano suit I had shoved into the back of the dresser.

Hmmmmm. Time for Plan B. If I could think of a Plan B.

"My stomach hurts!" I blurted out. "Must have been something I ate."

Polly snorted. "You haven't eaten yet," Polly reminded me.

"You're just hungry," Mom reasoned.

"So quit fooling around, and let's go!" Dad said.

I had no choice. It was Sink or Swim time.

And I knew which one I was going to do.

On our way to the Atlantis pool, I spied that weird guy with the bucket that I had seen yesterday. The guy who warned me that Club Lagoona was dangerous. As I passed him, he paused and picked up a piece of litter.

"Watch out for the deep end," he muttered. Then he scurried away.

What am I supposed to be watching for? I wondered. If this guy was playing some kind of game, it wasn't funny!

But I couldn't think about him. I had bigger problems on my mind. In a few minutes, the fact that I couldn't swim would be out in the open. My mom, my dad, and my obnoxious sister were going to witness my humiliating plunge to the bottom of the pool.

But then something great happened!

"Okay, everyone!" a Club Lagoona lifeguard shouted through a megaphone. "For the Sink or Swim race we'll be separating into groups. Afterward, you'll be put into smaller groups according to your skill. Ladies, follow Tina!" A woman with a long blond ponytail waved.

"Gentlemen, you'll be swimming with Philip!" the lifeguard continued. A dark-haired guy raised his hand.

"Girls, with Dave. Boys, with Barry," the lifeguard finished.

My family would be down at the other end of the pool, I realized. I was so relieved, I almost kissed Polly.

Almost.

"See you, squirt!" I told her cheerfully. I jogged over to join my group.

Barry wore his "Barracuda" top again. Something about the guy bugged me. I thought back to the day before. Why would an instructor shove a poor, unsuspecting kid into the water?

Barry nodded at me, then blew a whistle. My group jumped into the pool. Even me.

Ugh! I hate getting wet.

I clung to the side of the pool. I watched as the others splashed away from me. I figured I would do my usual trick of walking on the bottom and stroking my arms as if I were swimming. It always worked before!

But not this time! As soon as I let go of the side of the pool, I realized we weren't in the shallow end! I frantically stretched my legs, trying to touch bottom. It was no good. I was in way over my head.

I thrashed my feet. I doggie-paddled. It was awful. Everyone was ahead of me and I kept swallowing the water they were kicking up.

Then I realized I wasn't alone. There were two other guys doing the doggie paddle too. We were the last in the group to make it to the other side.

"You three," Barry called. "You're in my class—the Guppy class."

Oh, well. At least we didn't sink.

We crawled out of the pool and slunk to the shallow end. I sat between the two other Guppies. One of the guys was tall, even taller than me. The other kid was kind of chubby. He had on trunks exactly like mine. I guess his mom hit the gift shop too.

I smiled at them. "I'm Tad," I said.

The tall kid grinned. "Let me guess. They call you Tadpole."

I nodded. "Yeah. That's my stupid Club Lagoona name. What's yours?"

"Even worse." He lowered his voice. "My name's Neal. So they call me Eel."

"Don't worry," I reassured him. "I'll stick to Neal." I turned to the chubby kid. "How about you?"

"Mark," he replied.

"Shark!" Neal and I guessed together.

"You got it," Mark the Shark admitted. He sighed. "This place gives me the creeps."

"Me too," I agreed. "Hey, has a weird little guy with a bucket—"

But before I could finish, Barry shouted, "Okay, Guppies, *let's get wet!*"

Neal, Mark, and I glanced nervously at one another. Then we slowly slid into the pool.

Very slowly.

Barry started by having us stick our faces in the water. "Get used to *getting wet!*" he explained.

The next step was to open our eyes underwater.

"Okay, Tadpole, your turn." Barry stood in front of me. "When I say so, go underwater. Then open your eyes and count how many fingers I'm holding out. Got that?"

I nodded.

"Go!" Barry commanded.

I ducked underwater and opened my eyes. I blinked a few times. The saltwater burned, but after a moment I got used to it. Barry's hand came down. He held out three fingers.

I was about to push back up, when something behind Barry caught my attention. Something moving. Something green.

I peered past Barry's hand. The water made everything a little blurry.

Whatever it was had vanished.

I was running out of air. I surfaced, gasping for breath.

"How many fingers, Tadpole?" Barry asked.

"Three," I replied.

I scanned the pool. What *was* that green thing? And where had it gone?

Neal and Mark each took their turns counting fingers. I watched their expressions as they came up. Neither one seemed to have noticed anything unusual underwater.

Had I imagined the green thing? Probably just another piece of seaweed, I guessed.

Next, Barry stood a few feet away from the side of the pool. We had to push off from the side and swim underwater to him.

"If I start to drown, you'll save me, won't you?" I murmured to Neal and Mark. I was only half kidding.

"If you don't have to save me first!" Neal joked back.

"Go!" Barry cried.

I took a deep breath and went under. I pushed my feet against the side of the pool. The force propelled me forward.

I glanced over to see how my fellow Guppies were doing. Mark's arms were flailing all over the place, but he was clipping through the water.

Neal's face twisted with effort. But he cruised along too.

Then I saw it again. Something green.

Something that looked like a long green tentacle.

And it was reaching for Neal!

I broke through the surface of the water. I shook my head, spraying water everywhere.

"What's the matter, Tadpole?" Barry called. "Did you run out of air?"

"No! I—I—" My eyes darted around the pool. What creature could be so huge that it had a tentacle that long?

A gigantic sea monster would have a tentacle that long. But if there were a giant sea monster in the pool, I reasoned, we would all see it.

Wouldn't we?

Neal and Mark stood beside Barry. None of them seemed worried. None of them had seen what I had seen. Which made me wonder: Had I really seen it?

Forget it, I told myself. You're just afraid. And you're letting your imagination run away with you. I spent the rest of the lesson actually having fun. Neal and Mark were cool guys. Even Barry wasn't so bad—once you got used to him.

"Okay," Barry announced. "That's it for today."

A lifeguard rushed over to tell Barry he had a phone call. "I'll see you all tomorrow," he called as he dashed off toward the resort lobby.

I rubbed my head with my towel. I was feeling pretty good. I made it through a swimming lesson.

"That wasn't so terrible," Neal declared.

"Yeah," Mark agreed. "I think I'll even come to the next lesson. Hey, if you guys want to hang out later, come by. I'm in room one hundred four."

"Okay!" Neal replied. I nodded.

"Adios, fellow Guppies," Mark said. Then he slung the towel around his neck and jogged away.

I said good-bye to Neal and headed back toward my room. I felt a little silly about imagining a green-tentacled monster in the pool. Maybe I had been reading too many horror stories about the sea. My mom always says I have a "vivid imagination."

That's when I spotted my sister. She ran toward me.

Her eyes were enormous!

She was soaking wet and shaking.

She jumped up and down.

"The creature!" she blurted out. "I saw it!"

6

I knew it! There *was* something in the pool!

I grabbed Polly by the shoulders. "You saw it? You actually saw the creature?" I shouted.

"Yeah!" she cried. She hopped from one foot to the other.

"Was it big?" I asked.

"Massive!" she agreed.

"Was it green?" I demanded. I had to be sure I wasn't imagining things.

She stopped and thought a minute. "Yeah, it was mostly green. And it had this long tail and an enormous mouth."

"You got close enough to see *that?*" I asked in disbelief.

"Of course," she insisted. "I rode down on the tail,

and it spat me right out of its mouth into this whirlpool! It was amazing, Tad. You have to try it! You just have to!"

Now I realized which creature she was talking about.

"It was unbelievably cool! I slid down three times already. And I'm going back for more!"

Yup. I should have known. She was talking about the famous Creature Water Slide. The one I'd seen the kids on the day we arrived.

"You have to try it, Tad! It's the best water slide in the whole world!" she exclaimed.

"Yeah," I agreed weakly. "Can't wait."

The whole family had dinner in Club Lagoona's Fishbowl Restaurant. Okay. I admit it. It was pretty incredible.

The floor of the restaurant was covered with fine white sand. Plants and trees grew everywhere. The walls were glass. Behind the glass swam all kinds of fish. It was as if we were eating in a giant fishbowl— only *we* were the fish!

I thought of my pet hermit crab back home in his terrarium. Now I knew how he felt!

It gave me the creeps. I couldn't shake the feeling that I was having dinner underwater. And I could swear some of those fish glared at me!

While we ate our meal, sharks swam by. We were

stared at by giant sea turtles, manta rays, and tiny puffer fish.

"Look!" Polly cried, dropping her spoon. "It wants a kiss!"

A giant grouper pressed its mouth against the glass right behind us.

"Go on, Polly!" Mom urged. "Give him a kiss!"

Polly jumped out of her seat and darted over to the glass. She pressed her lips against the grouper's. The grouper backed up and quickly swam away.

"Smart fish," I commented.

Everyone laughed—even Polly. Mom and Dad were in really good moods. They were obviously enjoying Club Lagoona as much as Polly.

"How did your lesson go today, Polly?" Dad asked. Ice cubes shaped like sea horses floated around inside his bright green drink. He took a sip.

"It was great!" Polly answered. "I made lots of new friends. Mostly we practiced the backstroke. My teacher said I was a natural."

"How about you, Tad?" Mom asked. "Did you make some new friends?"

I nodded and sipped my Tropical Lagoona Shake. "Yeah, I met two guys."

"Bet you were the best in your class, eh, Tad?" Dad smiled broadly at me.

I tried to think of what to say. Maybe it was time to tell them about my fear of the water.

45

But they were so happy, I hated to spoil it. And I had to admit, I *was* starting to like the water. A little.

"Actually, there are three of us in my class who are about the same," I explained.

I'll tell them later, I decided. And maybe if I keep going to the swimming lessons, I'll improve. Who knows? I reasoned, maybe by the final Sink or Swim relay, I'll have nothing to confess.

After dinner we all split up. Mom and Dad went to Adult Recreation and Polly met some of her new friends.

I wasn't sure what to do. I found myself wandering back toward the Atlantis pool. Something seemed to pull me there.

The pool was deserted. A lone lifeguard sat atop a high chair, reading by the dim lights. He must be there to stop people from swimming after hours, I figured.

I glanced down toward the deep end. A strange figure headed my way. As he got closer, I realized it was the little guy with the bucket.

I began to feel nervous. I wasn't exactly sure why.

Should I go before he spots me—and gives me another weird warning? I wondered. Or should I stay and see what he's up to? Maybe ask him about the green thing in the pool.

Before I could decide, he was right beside me. But he didn't look at me. Instead, he gazed into his bucket. "You know more than you realize," he whispered.

"Huh?" I asked. "What do you mean? What do I know?"

He continued past me.

I turned and watched him. Was he talking about the monster in the pool? And if he knew about it, why wasn't he *doing* anything?

I ran after him. I had to know more.

I saw him dash around a corner.

"Wait!" I called. "I have to talk to you—"

I rounded the corner.

He was gone.

He'd disappeared into thin air!

I stopped abruptly. My mouth dropped open. "Where . . . ? How . . .?" I muttered. How could he have vanished?

My eyes searched the area. I spotted the sign for the games arcade. It was a giant fish that blew bubbles with the words GAMES! GAMES! GAMES! flashing in pink neon.

Maybe the strange little guy ducked in there!

I dashed over to the arcade. I was determined to find the man and ask him some questions.

I crossed the threshold of the arcade. Instantly the blaring sounds of video, computer, and virtual reality games blocked out everything else. The little man was nowhere in sight.

I glanced around, searching for him. Lights flashed

all around me. The place was packed with shouting kids. It was useless, I realized. I didn't see the guy anywhere. I would have to find him tomorrow.

I strolled through the crowded arcade.

My eyes locked on a game that was shaped like a big booth. The words UNDERWATER TERROR 2 blinked from the top of it.

Since I was already there, I might as well try the game. It *was* supposed to have the most awesome graphics—*and* be more realistic than any other game in the world.

Besides, I already mastered Underwater Terror 1. I was sure to beat this game in no time.

Finally, I thought. Something I'm good at— something where I don't have to swim!

As I approached the booth, I glanced around again for the little man.

I really wanted to talk to him. I had to find out why he acted so weird. And what he meant by all those warnings.

Because there was definitely something fishy going on at Club Lagoona!

7

The next morning I woke up really tired. In fact, I couldn't believe it was morning already. My sister and I were about to knock on our parents' door. Then I noticed a piece of paper taped to the doorknob.

"Hold on, Polly, there's a message," I told her. I pulled the note off and read it. "It says they went to the Rise and Shine Water Aerobics and they'll be back later."

Polly raised her eyebrows. "That's funny. Dad made a big deal about us coming to meet them." She shrugged. "Guess they changed their minds. Oh, well. See you later."

"Yeah, see you," I murmured. "Meet me back at our room before lunch. Okay?"

"Okay," she called as she dashed away.

I continued to stare at the note. Something about it bugged me. Then it hit me—the handwriting. It slanted the wrong way.

Mom didn't write like that.

Neither did Dad.

So who wrote the note?

I tried to shake off the creepy tingle along the back of my neck. A lot of weird things had happened since we arrived at Club Lagoona. The disappearing diver. The green thing in the pool. The little man with his warnings.

What was going on?

I felt disappointed that I didn't find the little guy last night. I bet he could have given me some answers.

I kept my eyes peeled for him as I trudged to my Guppy swimming lesson. But I never spotted him.

Mark and Neal were already in the pool when I arrived. I felt that familiar fear as I lowered myself into the water. But soon I was splashing and laughing just as much as my fellow Guppies.

Barry had us doing lots of fun things in the water. We even played a game of water polo in the shallow end.

As I gazed at the sparkling water, I started to think maybe I was being dumb. Of course there was no monster in the Atlantis pool! I was overreacting.

After the lesson, Mark, Neal, and I flopped on the side of the pool, each of us catching our breath.

"This place sure keeps you busy," I remarked. "I haven't seen my parents since last night."

"Did they go to that Rise and Shine Water Aerobics?" Neal asked.

I nodded.

"So did mine," Mark commented. "I wonder if they'll be back for lunch."

"Speaking of lunch, I'm starved!" I scrambled to my feet and stretched. "Catch you later."

Just then, Barry strolled over to us. "Hey, Guppies," he said. "I've decided you ought to have an extra lesson."

"Sorry, Barry," I apologized. "I promised I'd meet my sister."

"And my parents are expecting me," Neal told him.

Barry looked disappointed for a moment. Then he turned to Mark with a big grin on his face. "Looks like it's just you and me," he said.

Mark shrugged. "Sounds cool," he replied.

Barry's smile widened. "A private extra lesson. Just what you need." He clapped a hand firmly on Mark's shoulder.

"See you," Mark said.

"Later," Neal responded, and hurried to meet his parents.

All that swimming made me really ready for lunch. I said good-bye to Mark and Barry, then jogged back to the room to meet Polly.

She wasn't there.

I went ahead and changed and checked Mom and Dad's room again. They still weren't back.

Weird. Where could they have gone?

Maybe they were too hungry to wait. I guessed they were already having lunch.

I hurried to the Sand Bar. I scanned the dining room. But they weren't there.

I'm here, I told myself. I might as well eat. Who knows? Maybe they'll turn up.

After my burger and shake I decided to find Neal and Mark. Maybe they'd have some ideas about where everyone had disappeared to. Besides, I was feeling kind of lonely hanging out by myself.

I checked the Atlantis pool, but Mark wasn't around. I guessed his extra lesson with Barry had ended. Then I cruised around the resort, searching for Neal. I found him watching kids coming down the Creature Water Slide.

"Hey!" I called, jogging toward him.

He turned and waved at me. "What's up?" he greeted me.

"Not much. My family has disappeared," I said half jokingly.

Neal stared at me. "Mine too," he told me. "My parents never came back after water aerobics."

I felt that creepy tingle again.

Maybe I wasn't being silly. Maybe something was actually wrong.

"Let's find Mark and see if he knows anything," Neal suggested. "Maybe there's some activity all the parents went to."

"Good idea," I agreed. "He's not at the pool. Let's check his room."

Neal and I hurried to the cluster of suites near the reception lobby. We found the room, and I knocked on the door.

No answer. I knocked harder. Still nothing.

Neal and I gazed at each other.

We both knew his swimming lesson was over. I had just been over the whole club looking for Neal. I never came across Mark. So where was he?

Neal and I stood in front of his door, trying to figure out what to do.

Some kid came up behind us. "What are you two doing?" he demanded.

"We're looking for Mark Browning," I replied.

"Well, why don't you try his room?" the guy said.

"This *is* his room," I argued.

"No way." He opened the door with a key. "I checked in half an hour ago. This is *my* room. No one named Mark is in this room."

I stared at the number on the door again: 104.

"That was definitely Mark's room number," I said to Neal.

He nodded. "Maybe we should check with the front desk," he suggested. "Just to be sure."

We raced to the reception desk. "Could you tell me Mark Browning's room number?" I asked.

The girl behind the desk put down her nail file and tapped something into her computer. "There's no

Mark Browning registered at the Club Lagoona," she announced.

"Huh?" I glanced at Neal, then back at the receptionist. "That can't be right. We have swimming lessons together."

"Hey, I know," Neal piped up. "Maybe he's registered under his Club Lagoona name! Shark. Shark Browning."

She shook her head. "There is no one named Browning at all."

"But how can that be?" I protested. "He's here with his mom and dad."

"Yeah," Neal explained. "We just saw him a little while ago. And Mark told me they were staying until the end of the week."

She glanced back at her computer and tapped on the keyboard. Then she looked back up at us.

"There has never been anyone named Mark Browning registered here at the Club Lagoona," she repeated slowly.

She smiled.

"Not ever."

8

"She's wrong," Neal whispered as we walked down the hall. "Maybe she's new. Maybe she doesn't know how to work the computer."

"She seemed to know what she was doing," I replied. "She checked us in yesterday."

"Well, maybe there's some glitch with the computer, Tad. After all, people don't just disappear, do they?" Neal demanded.

"No," I answered. "They don't."

"The last time we saw Mark was when Barry wanted to give him the extra lesson," Neal said. "But he could be anywhere in the club now!"

"But that wouldn't explain why he's not in the computer!" I argued.

Neal shrugged.

"Okay, let's say we had the wrong room number," I reasoned. "Got it backward or something."

Neal nodded.

"That would explain the guy in Mark's room. And," I continued, thinking rapidly, "let's say there was a computer foul-up."

"It happens all the time to my dad," Neal offered.

"But that doesn't explain why my sister didn't meet me back at the room. Or where our parents are."

"Umm . . ." he murmured. "Okay, there has to be a logical explanation."

I stared at him, waiting. I was stumped.

He snapped his fingers. "Maybe your sister is with the adults doing some boring exercise class or something."

I shook my head. None of it made sense.

"I'm going to phone home," I announced.

Neal looked surprised. "Why?" he asked. "No one's there."

"Maybe my parents had to go home. Maybe there was some kind of emergency and they didn't have time to tell us. Or maybe they didn't want us to worry."

"Don't you think you're overreacting?" Neal suggested.

56

"I have to do something, and it's the only thing I can think of!" I snapped.

Maybe I *was* freaking out over nothing, but too many weird things had been happening to just be coincidences.

"Okay. Okay," Neal agreed. "I'll go with you."

I had to talk to somebody outside Club Lagoona. I had to make them understand the danger we might be in. They could find my family. They could come and get me out of here.

Neal and I pooled our change and headed toward reception. The same girl sat behind the desk.

"Where's a phone?" I blurted out.

She studied me closely. "You again," she said. "The phone's over there." She pointed with her nail file at a phone booth. It was on the other side of the lobby.

We raced over. There was no time to waste. I'd try my home phone first. If no one answered, I'd phone my next-door neighbor.

I dropped my money in and dialed. But instead of ringing, a voice came on the line.

"Hey, what's a fish like you doing out of the water?" a voice whined. "This is Club Lagoona. Now, get that bathing suit on, and *let's get wet!*" Then there was this crazy laughter.

I slammed the phone down. I waited a moment, then picked up the receiver to try again.

57

"Let's get wet! Let's get wet!" the voice screamed in my ear.

I held it up to Neal's ear. His eyes widened.

"Let's get out of here!" I gasped.

Two big hands clamped down on our shoulders from behind.

"Not so fast, Guppies!"

Neal and I froze. I gazed up into Barry's face.

"Time for you two to have an extra lesson," he informed us. His voice was low and serious. His fingers dug into my shoulder.

"N-n-now?" I stammered.

"We were just going to—" Neal began to protest.

Barry cut him off. "Now, Guppies. Let's go."

Barry marched us down to the pool like a couple of prisoners!

The Atlantis pool was crawling with Club Lagoona staff. I had never seen so many in one place before. They gathered around the pool, watching us closely.

"Okay, Guppies, *let's get wet!*" Barry bellowed.

The staff peered at us silently. I wanted to bolt. But there was no way to escape. We were surrounded.

I tried to stall. "Mark's not here," I declared.

"He already had an extra lesson," Barry reminded me. "Now, hop in!"

I stared at Barry. Something terrifying hit me.

The last time we saw Mark he was with Barry. Then he vanished.

Could Mark's disappearance be connected to his extra lesson?

I glanced at the staff positioned around the pool. They never took their eyes off us. As if they were waiting for something to happen.

But what?

I tried another tactic. "I have a cramp in my leg," I lied. I reached down and punched my calf. I grimaced.

No good.

"You'll be fine." Barry sounded impatient. "Get in the pool and walk around."

I slid slowly into the water.

"Here. Put these on," Barry commanded. He threw masks and flippers to us.

"Why do we need these?" Neal asked. He glanced at the silent staff members lined up along the sides of the pool.

"You're diving for weights today," Barry explained. "Now, hurry up and get them on."

I grabbed a pair of flippers. They felt heavy even in the water. I struggled to pull them on. They were hard and uncomfortable. I stretched the strap across my heels.

"Mine are too tight," I complained.

Barry rolled his eyes. "They're adjustable, Tadpole. Now, hurry. You're holding us up."

The flippers felt really funny. Like I had frog feet. I practiced walking in them. I had to lift my legs way up.

I slipped on the mask. It covered my eyes and nose.

Barry stood at the side and tossed in a weight. We were going to take turns diving for it and bringing it back up.

I went first. I ducked underwater where the weight sank. It was amazing what I could see by wearing the mask. Neal's legs and feet. They looked kind of pale blue.

Just like what the shark sees in *Jaws,* I thought, shuddering.

I kicked my feet. Whoa! The flippers sent me across the shallow end unbelievably fast. Two kicks and I was right above the weight.

I reached down for it—and something in the deep end caught my eye.

Two kids hovered at the bottom of the pool. They wore bright red bathing suits and scuba gear.

In the deepest part.

They stood on top of something. I peered harder.

They were standing right on top of the biggest drain I'd ever seen!

The sight of the drain made me remember my tooth disappearing down the drain in my bathtub. *This*

61

drain was big enough to suck down a lot more than a tooth.

A familiar whirring sound startled me. The same whirring I heard when the diver disappeared. When that horrible green thing appeared in the pool.

I watched, stunned, as the drain slid open!

The current in the pool changed. I could feel myself being sucked toward the open drain. My heart pounded triple-time.

I saw the divers kick crazily. But their flippers were no match for the huge, sucking drain. As hard as they fought the current, they just stayed in one place.

I watched in terror as something slinked out of the open drain. A long green tentacle! It waved through the water like a piece of giant, slimy seaweed.

One kid must have seen it. His arms and legs started moving like crazy. He grabbed the other kid by the arm and pointed at the tentacle. Then both of them started swimming furiously. Desperately.

But it was useless.

The tentacle danced around them playfully. Then it struck. It whipped around both the divers so tightly, they were lashed together.

It dragged them straight down into the drain!

A moment later they were gone!

10

Horrified, I stared at the drain. One minute two kids played at the bottom of the pool. The next minute they vanished!

My entire body went stiff with fear. And then I felt the force of the drain pulling me toward it.

If I didn't do something fast, I'd be sucked in too!

Terror shot me into high gear.

I planted my feet firmly on the rough pool bottom. I squatted down like a frog in my flippers. I pushed as hard as I could and kicked my legs.

I zoomed straight up. I heard the whirring sound again and felt the force from the drain weaken.

The drain must be sliding shut! I realized.

I escaped!

I broke through the surface with a splash. I gasped

for air. I spotted Neal on the other side of the pool. I paddled furiously toward him. I had to warn him. We had to get out of the pool!

With the help of the flippers, I was beside Neal in an instant. "You've got to listen to me, Neal," I begged. "We're in danger!"

Neal gasped. "What are you talking about?" he demanded.

Before I could explain, Barry blew his whistle.

"Okay, you two, time to get into the deep end," Barry shouted.

"What?" My voice shook with fear.

I had to tell Barry what I had seen. The terror in the deep end. I turned to face him.

"That's right, Tadpole. The deep end," Barry repeated slowly. He stared at us, his eyes gleaming.

My whole body trembled. I realized something— something horrifying!

Barry *knows*. He knows exactly what's waiting for us in the deep end of the pool!

"Bet you two Guppies can't swim all the way down to the bottom and touch the drain," Barry teased.

My mouth opened to shout a warning. But before I could get a word out, Neal tucked and disappeared underwater.

No!

I had to stop him!

I gulped some air and pushed hard off the side.

64

I spotted Neal just ahead of me. He swam straight down, heading for the drain.

I kicked hard and stretched my arms to make big strokes. I was gaining on him. A few more strokes and I'd be able to grab his foot.

I nearly swallowed water with my next stroke. The noise was back! The whirring sound that meant the drain was sliding open.

And Neal was swimming right for it!

I strained every muscle to catch up. I snagged his flipper and held tight.

The drain finished sliding open. The whirring noise stopped.

The force of the drain dragged us down. As we were pulled closer, water whipped around like a whirlpool.

I lost my grip on Neal.

We tumbled and whirled. Spinning in smaller and smaller circles. Faster and faster.

We were headed straight down the drain!

As we tumbled helplessly through the water, Neal latched on to my ankle. He gripped me so tightly, it hurt. I glanced down.

It wasn't Neal!

It was—the *tentacle!*

It curled around me, pulling me down into the open drain. I clutched the side of the drain, but my fingers slid off.

Then I saw Neal. He circled above me, whipped

around in the whirlpool. The tentacle hadn't grabbed him.

I reached down to my ankle and grabbed the slimy thing. I squeezed as hard as I could. Suddenly it let me go!

I was free!

I tried to scramble out of the drain. But then the tentacle grabbed me around the shoulders. I felt something slam against my back. Neal and I were lashed together in the powerful grip of the tentacle.

It dragged us down into the drain into a long, twisting tunnel. We hurtled through, slamming against the sides.

My lungs burned.

Air! I need air! I thought desperately. My chest is going to explode!

Dark spots whirled around me, closing in on me.

I'm drowning! I realized.

Then everything went black.

My nose itched. I opened my eyes. A hard, round brown thing pressed against my face. I moved my head slightly.

I stared at a large coconut. My body lay sprawled on the edge of a lake.

I sat up slowly. My swimsuit was still soaked. Sand stuck to my face and body.

A nearby bush full of red flowers shook violently.

I scrambled to my feet, ready to run.

"Is that you, Tad?" a voice called from the bush.

Neal!

I let out a huge sigh of relief. "Are you okay?" I asked. I picked my way through the tangled roots and vines toward the bush. Shells crunched under my feet.

Neal crawled out slowly. "Yeah, I'm fine. But what happened? Where are we?"

I glanced around. Palm trees and tropical plants surrounded us. Above us was blue sky. "It looks like a jungle," I reported.

Neal rubbed his head. "We were swimming in the bottom of the Atlantis pool, by the drain," he remembered. "Then something grabbed us, and we were pulled through some sort of tube. I thought I was drowning!"

I nodded. "Me too. But how did we end up here?"

Neal shook his head. "More important, *where* is here?"

"Only one way to find out," I figured. We decided to explore. Tall bushes, spiky plants, and gnarled tree roots surrounded us.

Thwack! "Ouch!" I yelped. A thick, heavy leaf whacked me in the face.

"Yikes!" Neal cried. He stumbled over a low vine.

I found a stick and tried to beat a path through the thick vegetation. Neal followed. Sweat beaded up on my forehead.

Tough work!

After a while Neal took a turn beating back the plants.

"Shh!" I grabbed his arm to stop him.

"What?" Neal whispered.

We stood dead still and listened.

"Voices," I murmured. I pointed in the direction

they seemed to be coming from. We crept on our hands and knees through the thick underbrush.

I peered through the bushes into a small clearing. I could see bright colors: purple and orange, red and lime green. Were they flowers? Birds?

No! They were bathing suits! My parents' bright, ugly bathing suits!

I leapt up. "Mom! Dad!" I screamed.

They turned around as I pushed through the bushes. But my parents weren't alone! Everyone who vanished from the pool stood in the clearing. Polly, Mark and his family, the two kids in scuba gear. Even the diver from the first day.

"Neal!" a man called.

Neal followed close on my heels. "Dad! Mom!" he cried as we stumbled out of the thick undergrowth.

After we all hugged one another, everyone started chattering at once.

"The creature!" Polly's high voice rose above the rest. "In the deep end! It's horrible. It pulled us down the drain!"

"Shh." Mom squeezed Polly tight. "It's over now. It's gone. We're all here. We're together and safe."

We were together, all right. But I wasn't so sure about the safe part.

"We've got to find a way out of here," I declared.

"We searched around this area for one," Dad told me. "But we haven't had any luck yet."

"Well, let's search some more," I suggested.

Dad agreed. He nodded. "Everyone, stay together," he called.

I gripped my stick. Dad and I led the way.

Whack! I sliced at the thick undergrowth. We moved through the jungle slowly in a long line.

Whack! We trudged silently along. The jungle seemed to stretch on forever.

Thunk! I hit something. Something big and hard. I stopped. Neal banged into me from behind.

"What was that?" Dad shouted.

"I don't know," I answered. The thick plants and vines completely hid whatever it was I smacked. I prodded it with my stick. "There's something solid."

I reached out my hand and felt through the plants. "It feels like a wall," I told the others. "A straight glass wall."

They gathered around me.

"Maybe it's a house!" Polly cried. "Maybe someone lives here who can help us."

We tried to pry the plants apart. "It's cold and smooth," Neal's mom commented. "I think it's glass."

"It's glass all right," Dad said, rubbing his hand along it.

I leaned into the glass and tried to look through it. All I could see was blue on the other side.

"Something's moving in there!" Mom warned.

A bright blue and yellow fish swam past us.

"Is it a gigantic fish tank?" Neal asked.

"Maybe." Mom sounded very uncertain.

I looked up. Way, way above my head I could see the top of the wall—and the water line. Above that, I saw blue sky.

Another fish darted by.

A terrible suspicion filled my head. One I couldn't shake.

I thought back to the dinner we had at Club Lagoona. That night we also watched fish swimming by. It made me feel as if *we* were the ones in the tank.

Could the same thing be happening now?

"I think we should keep exploring," Dad recommended. He sounded nervous. "That glass wall is very, very high, and I don't think we'll find any help on the other side."

"Yes. Let's continue," Neal's dad agreed. He sounded nervous too.

We turned away from the mysterious glass wall and trudged through the jungle again. No one spoke.

The only sound was the *whack, thwack, thwack* of my stick as it hit the bushes.

Ka-thunk! I stopped. "I've hit another wall," I shouted to the others.

"What on earth?" Mom murmured.

"Are we trapped inside something?" Neal's mom asked. Fear made her voice tremble.

We stared at one another. No one had any answers.

We continued on. And it happened again.

We hit another wall. And this one *wasn't* covered by

plants and vegetation. We could see it clearly. And we could see what was on the other side.

Dark blue water.

"It's just like the other two," Mark's dad remarked. "Glass."

"Yeah," Polly added. "And just as high." I could tell she was about to cry.

"We're underwater," Neal whispered.

I realized what was going on. I had no doubt about it now.

"I think we're stuck inside a terrarium," I told the others. "Kind of like the Fishbowl Restaurant at Club Lagoona. We're in a giant terrarium in the middle of the ocean."

"But how? Why?" Everyone fired questions at me.

My dad held up his hands. "I came to the same conclusion as Tad. There are four glass walls surrounding us. Keeping us in here," he said. "And the question isn't how we got here. The question is—"

"How are we ever going to get out!" Mom finished for him.

"I guess we all just have to keep looking," I suggested.

I gazed at the faces surrounding me. Everyone wore terrified expressions. But they nodded.

I squinted my eyes and peered through the glass. It was deep blue. Way, way above my head I could make out what must be the waterline. The terrarium was only partly submerged in the water. Even if it was a long way up.

I opened my mouth to tell the others—when something appeared on the other side of the glass.

Something huge.

Something round.

Something hideous.

An enormous *eyeball*.

And it was staring right at me!

12

"**A**aaaaaahhh!" I shrieked. I leapt backward and banged into Neal. He clutched my elbow and gasped in fear. Everyone stumbled away from the wall.

"It's the creature," I whispered hoarsely.

The eyeball was a sickly yellow color. It was bigger than my dad! The creature was so huge, only a small part of its body was visible.

But what we could see was terrifying!

The creature was green and scaly, and seemed to be covered with slime. Below the eye was the creature's huge sucking mouth. It pulsed open and shut, open and shut. When it opened, rows of needlelike teeth glittered.

I shuddered.

Suddenly the creature's mouth opened wide. A long green tentacle shot straight out!

Smack! It slapped against the glass with a loud thud and latched on.

We all watched frozen in fear as hundreds of suckers on the tentacle fastened to the glass.

The creature's tentacle-tongue crept up the glass wall!

"It's trying to get in!" someone shouted.

"Run for it!" Neal screamed.

I stared at the gigantic, gross tongue as it inched its way up the smooth glass.

Sluurp! Sluurp! Sluurp! Slurrp!

"It's at the top!" Polly shrieked. "It's getting in!"

"Run!" Dad hollered. Everyone scattered, racing away from the glass wall and the monster on the other side.

But I couldn't move. All I could do was stand and stare as the tentacle-tongue waved in the air over my head.

The suckers squeezed open and shut, trying to latch on to something.

The tentacle extended farther. It lashed through the air blindly.

A terrible smell filled my nostrils. Like brussels sprouts mashed up in dog food. Curtains of green slime dripped from the tentacle and showered over me.

75

"Aaaahh!" I shrieked. The green slime oozed over my bare arms.

Then something wrapped around my wrists.

I fought back, desperate to shake it off.

"Stop, Tad! It's me!"

I turned. The tentacle didn't have me. It was Dad, trying to drag me out of the creature's path.

I lost my footing and fell into a ditch. Dad fell in on top of me.

I lay under him, listening to the horrible slurping. I tried not to breathe in the sickening smell.

Slime dripped onto us as the tentacle-tongue passed over our hiding place. Luckily we were jammed deep into the ditch and the tentacle couldn't get a grip. It kept moving.

I heard shrieks and shouts. Dad popped his head up, and I peered out from under him.

The tentacle lashed back and forth wildly. Then it wrapped itself around Mark, his mom, and his dad. It lifted them off the ground. We heard their terrified screams as the tentacle hoisted them high in the air!

Everyone raced out of their hiding places. We had to help them!

I picked up a stone and aimed at the tentacle. It missed. We all tossed rocks and stones. I tried again and hit one of the suckers.

But it seemed only to infuriate the creature. It lashed more violently, whipping Mark and his parents around above us.

"It's taking them!" Mom screamed.

We all watched helplessly as Mark and his family were yanked over the top of the glass wall. We peered horrified through the glass as they were dragged into the water, and down through it. Then they vanished as the creature sank out of view.

"Noooooo!" Polly screamed.

I clutched my stomach. I felt as if I were going to faint.

But the worst was yet to come.

Crruncch! Crrunccch! Crunnnccch!

We stared at one another. We all knew what the sickening sound meant.

"It's eating them!" Polly shrieked. "The creature is eating them all!"

13

Polly couldn't stop screaming. "It's eating them! And we're next!"

Mom tried to calm her down. It wasn't working.

I shook all over. My whole body felt numb. It was as if my brain couldn't grasp what my eyes had just seen.

"We're not safe here," Dad determined. "We're too close to the side of whatever kind of tank we're in."

"He's right," Neal's dad said. "We need to get away from these walls. We should head to the middle of the tank."

We walked quickly for quite a while. No one spoke a word. We were all too freaked out to talk. The only sounds were the leaves and plants softly squashing under our feet.

"This must be near the center," I announced finally.

"Right," Dad agreed. "Everyone stay together here in this clearing." He looked at Neal's dad. "We'll go find some food. That way, we'll be able to stay here in the middle for a while. The rest of you, don't move. We'll be right back."

We watched the two dads disappear into the bushes.

"We should be searching for a way out!" I complained. Soon, the dads came back with some fruit. It looked like tiny pineapples.

I rolled my eyes. How could anyone think about eating at a time like this?

I kicked at the dirt in frustration. I felt more than ever that we couldn't stop now. We had to find a way to escape.

I glanced at the group. Everyone sat in a circle, dividing the fruit. No one paid any attention to me. This was my chance.

I slipped away.

I followed our path back to where the creature had snatched Mark and his family. I decided to start there and go right around the wall. Maybe I could find a ladder—or some other way out.

My heart pounded faster as I approached the spot where the creature had been. I didn't want it to find me, so I dropped to my knees and began to crawl through the bushes.

I found the glass and decided to go to the right. I scanned the surface of the glass. I didn't even know what I was looking for. An opening. A door. Anything that wasn't just flat, smooth glass.

I crawled slowly, feeling every bit I could reach. I peered up along the wall, straining to see what was above me.

Every now and then a fish swam past. I tried not to freak out when I saw something.

I knew the creature could appear at any time. I knew it could latch on to the glass and heave its huge tentacle-tongue right over the side.

But I had to go on. It was up to me.

After about twenty minutes, I'd turned two corners. I realized there was probably only one more wall to explore.

I was beginning to doubt that there was an exit. Maybe we'd just been thrown into the tank by the creature. Maybe it was storing us there until it was hungry. I thought of lobsters I'd seen in restaurants, swimming in tanks, waiting for a hungry diner to pick them out and eat them.

Now *we* were the lobsters!

I paused and glanced around. I realized I was nearly back where I'd started.

I knew the others would have missed me by now. But I had to go on. Everyone's life depended on it.

As I turned the last corner, I spotted a huge green

sea turtle. It was swimming up to the wall, butting its nose softly on it.

I watched it swim around, as if it were trying to get in.

It went way up the wall. I could see its yellow undershell as it paddled up.

It kept butting its pointed snout on something.

I squinted hard.

High up the glass wall—there was a huge hose connected to the tank. Where the tank met the hose I could just make out—an opening!

I found an old dead palm tree and dragged it to the wall. I leaned it against the glass. It reached the hole!

I shinnied up slowly. As I got closer, I could see that on the other side of the glass the hole connected to a long black tube. The tube was so long that it twisted around the corner of the tank and out of sight.

Could it lead to the drain in the Atlantis pool?

My heart started pounding again. But this time it was with hope, not fear.

When I'd nearly reached the top, the sea turtle swam away quickly. It ducked under the tube and vanished around the corner.

I froze. Something must have frightened it away.

I was almost too afraid to look. Out of the corner of my eye I noticed a shimmering object moving toward me.

"On the count of three," I ordered myself.

The thing kept coming my way.

"One. Two. Three!" I shouted. I whipped my head around.

And stared into the face of a big fat eel!

"Ha!" I was so relieved it wasn't the creature that I laughed out loud. I felt the tree tip.

"Whoa!" I clutched the tree, steadying myself.

I was never so glad to see an eel in my life!

I hoisted myself up to the hole. It was the entrance to a tunnel! It had to be the one that Neal and I had hurtled through after we were sucked down the drain. It made sense, because I was nearly back at the spot where we'd all found one another.

Carefully, I pulled myself into the tunnel. I had to find out if I was right.

Maybe I had found the way out!

I crawled forward in the dark, cramped space. I knew I was surrounded by deep water on both sides. I tried not to let that thought get to me.

I wanted to turn back. I couldn't see a thing. I started to sweat and feel trapped in the dark tunnel.

I stopped crawling.

I took a few deep breaths, trying to control the panic building up inside of me.

Then I saw it. A tiny point of bluish light!

There was definitely a light up ahead. It had to be the end of the tunnel.

I began crawling again, faster now. I wasn't going to

turn back. Wherever this tunnel led, I was nearly there.

I stopped to wipe the sweat off my forehead. It dripped into my eyes and burned.

Then I heard a noise. I listened hard.

It sounded like the whirring noise in the bottom of the Atlantis pool! But the whirring was drowned out by another sound. A low rumbling.

What was it?

The rumbling grew louder and louder.

I glanced back. Nothing but darkness. I couldn't even see the end where I'd started.

I faced forward again. Then I saw it. Through the long, dark tunnel, light from the other end reflected on something. Something racing toward me.

Water!

A gigantic wall of water!

Rushing right at me!

My scream echoed down the tunnel.

I tried to back up. I could see the water coming at me. I could hear it rushing. I could even smell it.

I scurried backward. But it was hopeless.

There was nothing I could do. I took a deep breath and ducked my head under my arms.

Whoosh!!!

The wall of water slammed into me.

Water rushed into my face. I clamped my eyes shut. The water poured into my ears and up my nose.

It threw me up against the top of the tunnel. My head pounded as if I'd been punched. I twisted and turned, hurtling backward, spinning out of control, tumbling and whirling.

I'm going to drown! I thought in terror. I'm going to drown in this tunnel.

Suddenly I felt a big bump. I sped over the ridge of the tunnel entrance. I flew through the air in a jet of water!

I pulled myself into a ball.

Wham!

I lay still for a moment, trying to catch my breath. Then I opened my eyes.

The first thing I saw was a coconut.

I was right back at where I landed with Neal! Back at where we found ourselves after being sucked down the drain in the Atlantis pool. But where was the water? I dug through the dirt and found a small drain. The water must get out through that, I realized.

My whole body ached. I checked quickly for injuries. Just a couple of nasty scratches. I scrambled to my feet.

I had to find the others. I had to tell them what I found. This tunnel must be the only way out.

But it was useless if we couldn't get past the rushing waves of water.

Well, I reasoned, I found the exit. Let someone else figure out how to handle the water problem!

Smack!

I spun around at a sound. My eyes widened.

"No!" I whispered hoarsely.

The huge green tentacle pressed against the wall.

Sluurp. Sluurp. Sluurp. Sluurp.

The creature was back!

The tentacle crawled its way up the wall.

The awful noises grew louder and faster as the tentacle picked up speed.

Slurp! Sluurp! Slurp! Sluurp!

My head tilted back as my eyes gazed up and up and up.

The huge green tentacle waved in the air above me. Green slime streamed off it. The suckers opened and closed. They wanted to grab something.

They wanted to grab me!

I flattened myself on the ground and closed my eyes.

Whap!

I felt something hit my back!

It had me!

The creature's suckers latched on to my body. They tugged my skin, pulling at it with an awful popping and sucking sound. The tentacle pinned my arms to my sides. It twisted around me.

Then it raised me high into the air.

Over the top of the terrarium.

I glanced down.

The hideous eye on top of the creature's huge head blinked at me. Its enormous scaly green body was dimly visible in the water.

It clutched me in its tentacle-tongue. But I could see that there were many other tentacles thrashing in the water below me!

My whole body went stiff with terror. I knew what was coming next.

It was going to eat me!

15

I was going to eat me!

"Noooooo!" I screamed. "You're not going to eat me!"

I kicked and wriggled in the tentacle. But its grip held me like a vise. It squeezed me so tight, I felt as if I were going to pop. I struggled against it with all my strength.

But the creature was so much stronger.

It lashed me violently through the air. The slimy suckers attached to my skin, pulling and twisting my flesh away from my bones! Each time the slippery suckers released me, a horrible wet *pop!* vibrated through me.

Then I noticed something. The gross slime oozing from the tentacle's suckers was like thick grease. My body was becoming slick and slippery.

Instead of pushing out against the tentacle, I tried slipping my arms up. I squirmed and wriggled like a worm on a hook. I twisted my body and slid my arms up my sides. Farther, farther.

Thwop!

I did it! I popped out of the creature's grip!

A moment later I landed with a thud on something hard. A coral reef! What luck! I would have a hard enough time fighting the creature on land! If I'd plopped into the water, I'd have been a goner for sure.

I stood up. My knees were scraped and sore from landing on the reef, but otherwise I was okay. I glanced around quickly. Was there any place to run? I had to put some distance between me and the creature!

Then I spotted a spray of water in the distance. It shot straight up in the air. I shaded my eyes.

Yes! The water must be from the fountain in the center of Club Lagoona! I was near the island! Maybe I could get help!

I raced toward it, running carefully along a high ridge in the center of the reef. Water lapped up both sides.

The surface was uneven, making it difficult to run. I tried to avoid the huge jagged barnacles that grew along the ridge. My breath came in gasps as I darted along the reef, terrified that the creature might grab me any second.

Suddenly my foot hit a slippery patch. I tumbled into the water.

The saltwater made my scrapes burn. I kicked back to the reef and tried to hoist myself up. The reef sloped sharply into the cold water.

I kept slipping back in. Back in to where the creature might be lurking.

I could picture its massive green body. Its gaping mouth with its razor-sharp teeth. Its slimy scales and disgusting tentacles and suckers.

I could still hear the sound of Mark and his family being eaten. That sickening *Crunch!*

I had to get out of the water!

I dog-paddled for a while along the side of the reef, frantically searching for a spot where I could haul myself back up.

Finally I found a place that wasn't so steep. I reached out with my arms. I kicked extra hard and pulled for all I was worth.

I made it! I was back up on the reef. Safe, at least for the moment.

I moved more carefully. I knew I had to watch out for the barnacles and the slippery patches.

I gazed toward Club Lagoona. I was nearly at the end of the reef. My mind raced. How will I attract attention? I thought frantically. How will I get help? Will I be able to find the huge tank I escaped from?

And where is the creature now?

I picked my way along the reef, knowing I'd soon have my answers.

I stumbled. The reef seemed to move slightly under my feet!

I tried to relax. I was exhausted and dizzy. I was imagining things.

I gazed straight ahead, hoping to see more land, a place to escape to. I noticed something new. The ground felt different under my feet. It seemed to be changing, getting softer.

Whoa! The reef really moved!

It wasn't my imagination! Not at all.

I gazed at the ground, wondering what was going on. There were fewer barnacles, I realized. The reef seemed more even, almost smooth. I had to slow down as I continued on.

A sudden violent shake made me stop dead in my tracks. I dropped to my knees.

Several more shakes followed.

"What's happening?" I cried.

My voice sounded tiny and scared.

Then I knew! I was on a tiny coral reef island. I was in the middle of an earthquake!

I had to get off the island fast. I had to get to someplace more secure.

I started to run again and slid all over the place. I fell and picked myself up again and again.

The shaking grew more violent!

I couldn't hold on much longer!

The ground rose beneath me, and I was lifted into the air! Higher and higher above the cold, rough water.

I gazed at the sea below and swallowed hard.

I tried to cling to the reef. It shifted beneath me. My feet slid on the soft, slippery surface.

Suddenly I knew. I was not standing on a reef.

This was no earthquake.

It was much, much worse!

16

"**A**aaahhhhhh!" I shrieked. The horrible truth sank in!

I was walking on the back of the creature!

The hideous single eye blinked far ahead of me. Below me, dozens of tentacles swirled around in the water.

I clung to the creature's back, riding it like a huge bucking bronco!

The creature was bigger than gigantic. I realized I'd seen only a tiny part of it before. Here, on top of it, the creature was much, much bigger than it looked through the glass.

Higher and higher into the air I soared as the creature heaved its enormous body. Club Lagoona was a tiny dot below me. Water dripped off the creature's back, splashing into the ocean.

My body shivered in fear. But at least while I was on its back, I was out of the reach of its tentacle-tongue!

Then the creature started sinking. I could see the surface of the water heading up toward me. The creature was submerging!

How could I escape? I asked myself. What could I do?

Terror froze my brain.

The creature lowered itself into the ocean. Water lapped around my ankles. My knees. My neck.

I was a goner!

Just as I was about to go under, a tentacle sneaked up from beneath the creature. It wrapped around my waist. The slimy suckers grabbed on to my skin. It lifted me high, high, higher!

Then the tentacle fell. I flew through the air—plunging toward the water. The wind whistled in my ears. I clung to the tentacle with all my might!

Smack!

I hit the water hard. It stung my skin like a terrible sunburn.

The tentacle released me. I went under, kicking and struggling, trying to fight my way back up to the surface.

Then I felt two tentacles grab me. One slipped

around each ankle! They lifted me out of the water. I felt like a wishbone at Thanksgiving!

I dangled upside down, far above the water. Higher than the high dive in the Atlantis pool!

Then the tentacles let go!

I tried to hold my body straight as I sailed through the air. I whipped my arms out in front of me to break my fall.

I plunged headfirst into the cold, churning water. It felt as if I'd been pounded by hundreds of fists.

The force of the dive plunged me deep into the water. I didn't think I could stop going down. I stretched my arms out, trying to slow myself.

Then I shifted my arms, hoping I could change direction. To go up. Finally, I turned. I kicked hard. I glimpsed the light of the surface above me.

I was almost there! I broke the surface and sucked in a breath of air.

But the tentacle grabbed me and yanked me down again!

The awful truth hit me. The creature was playing with me. Torturing me. The way my cat likes to torture its stuffed toy.

And once I was too tired to fight back, or it got bored, it would end it all. It would finally eat me.

No! I wasn't going to let it!

I struggled and kicked and hit the scaly thing. I yanked and pounded. It held me like a fist. It wrapped around my arms and squeezed.

I couldn't use my hands anymore. Now what? I refused to give up. I shook with disgust, but I couldn't think of anything else to do.

I opened my mouth wide. On the count of three, I told myself.

One. Two.

Chomp! My teeth dug into the tentacle.

Yuck! Bleehhh! A horrible taste filled my mouth.

And nothing happened. The creature didn't even seem to know I had bitten it.

I tried again. This time I aimed my mouth at a sucker. Maybe they would be more sensitive.

Chomp!

Ugh! The rubbery sucker wriggled in my mouth. Disgusting slime oozed into my mouth and down my chin.

The tentacle thrashed, but it didn't release me.

Another tentacle reached for my head and wrapped around it like a turban. The tentacles bound me up like a mummy. Then another tentacle floated in front of me.

Thwap! A gigantic sucker as large as my head landed square on my face.

I couldn't move. I couldn't breathe. I couldn't even see.

I was doomed!

17

I gathered the little bit of strength I had left. I couldn't give up. I had to make one last try.

I jerked my head from side to side wildly.

I kicked and squirmed and thrust my arms and legs out.

I opened my mouth and screamed harder and louder than I ever screamed in my whole life.

It worked.

When I opened my eyes, I wasn't drowning.

I wasn't even in the water.

I was in a dark and quiet room. Alone. I was sitting in a deep, comfortable chair.

I was okay!

I glanced down at myself.

The suckers! The creature's suckers were still all

over my body! I was still its prisoner! I tore at them, ripping them off me! Grabbing the wires and flinging them across the room. . . .

Wires?!

I realized I held something else in my hands too. A pair of strange-looking goggles.

"Hey, Tad, are you okay?"

Neal's voice, I realized, calling me from outside the room.

"Was that awesome or what?" Mark! Mark was there too!

But wait—I thought. The creature ate Mark and his whole family. Didn't it?

I sank back into the deep, comfortable chair and tried to think.

I remembered arriving at Club Lagoona, where everyone was water crazy. Okay.

Mark and Neal were my new pals from my swimming lessons. Images of the different club attractions flashed in my head: the Creature Water Slide. The Atlantis Swimming Pool. The neon *Games! Games! Games!* sign with the bubble-blowing fish.

But I couldn't remember anything else I did that night. And the next morning, strange things began happening. Crazy things went through my mind. A drain. A slimy green tentacle. A giant eyeball. Polly screaming.

I shook my head. What was real and what wasn't?

Then it hit me. I was in the arcade.

98

I'd been playing that virtual-reality game Underwater Terror 2.

I followed the weird little guy with the bucket into the games arcade. But then I lost him. As I searched the place for him, I found the game. And as I was about to play, I ran into Neal and Mark.

Yeah! It was all coming back to me!

I remembered Mark challenged Neal to a game of Aqua Doom. I found the virtual-reality game and decided to try it.

I remembered putting the virtual-reality glasses on and the voice saying, "Get ready for the water adventure of a lifetime!" The same thing I'd heard when we first arrived at the resort. I had to enter my Club Lagoona name and my room number. Then the game told me to put those electric suckers all over me.

I thought it was weird—I never had to do that for Underwater Terror 1—but the game wouldn't start until I put them on.

Yes, I told myself. And everything after that had all been a game.

I thought hard. So, what was real and what wasn't?

Club Lagoona? Weird but real.

Mom and Dad and Polly? Very real.

Neal and Mark? Definitely real.

Mark and his family being eaten? *Not* real. Whew!

I climbed out of the booth. Neal and Mark stood beside me now. They looked worried.

"Boy! You were screaming your head off! You okay?" Mark asked.

I laughed. "I am now."

"How was the game?" Neal asked.

"Awesome!" I replied truthfully. "Totally advanced graphics. It was *so* real." I gazed at them. "You guys were in it!"

"We were?" Neal shouted.

"This I have got to see!" Mark exclaimed.

"Hey, no time now," Neal interrupted. "The Sink or Swim relay starts in a few minutes.

"Go Guppies!" Mark shouted.

We all high-fived.

18

It was great to leave the dark arcade. The sun was blazing. Colors seemed even brighter than they had before.

"So, the virtual reality was scary, huh?" Neal asked as we walked over to the Atlantis pool.

"You got that right," I agreed.

"How did they put us in the game?" Mark wondered aloud.

"I think I know!" Neal answered. "Remember those pictures they took when we checked in?"

I thought back. Right. The receptionist snapped a photo of us on that first day.

"I asked them what they needed the pictures for," Neal explained. "They said they scan them into computers and use them for all sorts of stuff. Special buttons, T-shirts, signs." He grinned at me. "I guess they use them to scare us kids in virtual reality."

I kept staring at everything around me. It all seemed kind of unreal after the game.

Club Lagoona looked just the same. Only a little smaller. Even the Atlantis pool wasn't as big as in the game.

"Hey, Guppies, over here!" Barry shouted.

The sight of Barry and the Atlantis pool made me shudder. In the game, Barry was really evil. He sent us to the deep end even though he knew the creature would capture us.

I couldn't help but still feel a little afraid of him. Even though I knew he wasn't *really* a bad guy.

But I couldn't help thinking about the deep end. The whirring drain. The tentacle . . .

Snap out of it! I ordered myself. It was just a game!

I gazed around the huge pool area. People gathered on both sides of the pool. Banners and flags whipped brightly in the warm breeze.

"Hey, Tad, there's your family," Neal said. "They're sitting next to mine."

Neal and I waved. Mom, Dad, and Polly waved back.

The back of my neck tingled. I turned toward Mark. "Where are your parents?" I asked him.

"Eaten," Mark said.

"Huh?" I gasped.

"Eating," he shouted above the noise of the crowd. "I think they're still eating lunch."

"Oh," I muttered, feeling really stupid.

Then I remembered being scared by that mechanical shark and seeing the diver disappear.

I thought about that funny little man who kept giving me those warnings.

I remembered thinking the seaweed was some kind of monster with tentacles.

Boy, what a jerk *I* was!

Well, now that I had been scared out of my wits playing that game, *nothing* could bother me. I realized how silly all my fears were.

Including my fear of the water.

I gazed across the Atlantis pool. I felt very calm. I was even looking forward to the race.

That was a first! I realized. Me—eager to swim!

Barry lined us up for our relay. Me first. Then Neal. Then Mark.

I moved into the starting position Barry taught us. *Bang!*

I sprang from the side of the pool. The last thing I saw before I hit the water was the funny little man with his bucket of chlorine. Did he wink?

I cut into the water smoothly.

I could hear everyone in the crowd shouting.

"Go, Tad!" Polly's voice shrieked above all the others.

"You can do it, Tad!" Mom chimed in.

"Give it your best, Tad!" My father's voice boomed. "You're way in front! Keep going!"

I didn't worry about the swimmers in the other lanes. I focused on the end of the pool, where I would turn and go back to tag Neal.

I was nearly halfway across the pool now. I didn't feel tired. I felt happy, excited.

From the corner of my eye I noticed the swimmer in the next lane. Gaining on me as we neared the deep end.

I had to do something to keep my lead.

I ducked my head down and held my breath, and stroked as hard as I could.

Suddenly a noise met my ears.

A whirring noise.

A hideous whirring noise that sent shivers up my spine.

I peered through the water and saw a flash of green.

And I knew what was there.

I knew exactly what I would discover down in the deep end.

The giant drain at the bottom of the pool.

Sliding open.

And a slimy green tentacle slithering out. . . .

Only this time it was real.

This time I would really be face-to-face with the creature of Club Lagoona.

Are you ready for another walk
down Fear Street?
Turn the page for a terrifying
sneak preview.

R·L·STINE'S
GHOSTS OF FEAR STREET ® #22

FIELD OF SCREAMS

Coming mid-June 1997

The pitcher wound up. I tightened my grip on the bat. Then, from the corner of my eye, I caught a glimpse of the old man from the abandoned house on Fear Street. The one who scared me the day before. He stood at the fence. Watching me.

His eyes burned into mine. I felt as if I couldn't tear my gaze away from him.

What did he want?

"Duck!" someone yelled.

My head whipped around. Oh, man!

The ball was speeding straight toward me!

WHACK!

Pain exploded in my head. I saw a huge flash of white light. Little stars danced in front of my eyes.

I staggered. Dropped to the ground by home plate. When I hit the dirt, the thud echoed strangely in my ears.

Then everything went black.

The next thing I heard was someone calling my name.

"Buddy. Buddy, talk to me, son! Are you okay?"

I opened my eyes slowly. Man, did my head hurt!

My vision was blurry for a second. As it cleared, I made out faces peering down at me. Strangers.

"Are you okay, Buddy? That pitch hit you square in the head."

The man speaking was tall, with dark hair that he wore slicked back with some kind of shiny oil.

How does he know my name? I wondered fuzzily. I've never seen him before.

"Ooooh." I groaned and sat up slowly. My head throbbed where the ball had struck me. I felt dizzy.

"Thatta boy. Can you get up?"

Without waiting for an answer, he grabbed my arms and hauled me to my feet. I stood, wobbling for a second.

"Feeling steadier? Good. Shake it off," the man with the slicked-back hair told me.

Shake it off? I thought. I just got clobbered in the head with a fastball! Why aren't they rushing me to the hospital for a brain scan or something?

"Uh—I—" I started to say.

"Come on, tough guy!" he interrupted. "Take your base."

"But I—"

"You're fine. Take your base." The strange man tucked his hand under my elbow and hustled me to first base. "Good, good," he muttered, and trotted away.

Who was that guy, anyway?

I stood at first base and screwed my eyes shut, trying to get over my feeling of confusion.

"Batter up!" the umpire called.

I opened my eyes to see who was next at bat.

Then I stared.

Wait just one second! I thought. Who is *that* guy? He doesn't play on my team! And what's with his uniform?

The pants were baggy. The shirt was loose. The whole outfit looked like a sack. And instead of the red, white and blue colors of my team, it was white with black pinstripes.

Come to think of it, my own uniform felt weirdly heavy and loose. I plucked at the fabric with my fingers.

Black and white pinstripes!

My team didn't wear pinstripes!

Before I could think, the batter hit a grounder toward the shortstop. I took off from first base as the ball skipped past the shortstop and into the outfield.

I rounded second at full speed, really running

now. I slid into the bag and barely beat the throw to third.

I stood and brushed myself off. A rough hand clapped me on the shoulder.

"Way to go, Gibson," a deep voice said in my ear.

Gibson? Who was Gibson? I turned and found myself staring at a man with a heavy, red face. He had to be the third-base coach. Why else would he be standing there?

But I'd never seen him before, either.

What was going on?

Who were these people?

I was starting to get a really weird feeling. . . .

I licked my lips. "Saunders," I corrected. "My name is Saunders. Uh—who are you?"

The man laughed. "That's our Buddy. Always kidding around."

"Quit gabbing and get your heads in the game," the guy with the slicked-back hair yelled from across the field.

I peered at the next batter. You guessed it—someone else I didn't know. In fact, I couldn't find a single familiar face on the whole baseball diamond. Hank, Scott, Glen—they had all vanished!

It was the same with the people in the bleachers.

Total strangers, all of them. And they all wore funny clothes. For example, there wasn't a woman there without a hat on. And gloves. In the middle of summer!

And where were my parents? They had been there five minutes ago. But now I couldn't spot them anywhere.

The pitcher zoomed a fastball down the center of the plate. The guy at bat took a huge swing. He crushed the ball, sending it out of the park.

"Home run!" people screamed.

"What's the matter with you, Gibson? Don't just stand there. Run home!" the third-base coach urged.

Why did he keep calling me Gibson?

I ran to home plate. Then I trotted to the dugout. As I passed the fence, I caught a glimpse of the parking lot.

Whoa. A huge maroon roadster with an odd, rounded shape sat next to an old pickup truck. The roadster looked like it came from one of those old gangster movies. The truck was straight out of *The Beverly Hillbillies.*

"Uh, are we sharing the park with a classic-car show today?" I asked a freckled kid in the dugout.

He stared at me as if I was crazy. "What's a classic car?"

I started to feel really *scared.*

I could think of only one explanation for all this.

What if I really *was* crazy? What if that knock in the head had made me go insane?

My temple throbbed. I sat on the bench and rubbed my head.

"Are you okay? You don't look so hot," the freckled kid told me.

I'm not! I wanted to shout. I'm going nuts! Loopy! Losing my marbles!

But I was scared to say it out loud. What would they do to me? Cart me off to a loony bin?

"Head hurts," I mumbled at last.

I glanced down at the end of the dugout. A dozen strange, small gloves lay in a pile on the ground. They looked like pot holders. Leather pot holders. Not baseball mitts.

Nearby was a stack of wooden bats.

Wooden bats? Our team always used aluminum bats.

Didn't we?

I was still sitting there, trying to figure it all out, when the freckled kid poked me with a bat. "Get up, Buddy. Our side is retired."

"What?" I glanced up. Players in black-and-white pinstriped uniforms streamed past me to the pile of gloves. It was our turn in the outfield.

I must have looked uncertain, because the man with the slicked-back hair reached into the pile and pulled out a glove. He threw it to me. "Get out there, Gibson," he barked. "We haven't got all day."

I caught the glove and pulled it on as I ran for third. It looked small on my hand, but it seemed to fit okay. Someone had written *Gibson* on it in blue ink.

That name again. I knew it from somewhere, but where?

Then, suddenly, I remembered the old man from yesterday. The old man from the house on Fear Street. The one Hank thought was a ghost.

Gibson was the kid the old man told me about. Buddy Gibson. The kid in the photograph.

The photograph from 1948.

I stopped running and stood there with my mouth hanging open.

Could it be? Was it even possible?

It was the only explanation that made sense. Besides my being crazy, that is.

It explained why all the uniforms looked goofy. Why the gloves were weird and the caps were strange. Why everything seemed as if it came from an antique shop.

And why everybody kept calling me Gibson.

Somehow, I *was* Gibson.

Somehow, I'd gone back in time!

About R.L. Stine

R.L. Stine, the creator of *Ghosts of Fear Street,* has written almost 100 scary novels for kids. The *Ghosts of Fear Street* series, like the *Fear Street* series, takes place in Shadyside and centers on the scary events that happen to people on Fear Street.

When he isn't writing, R.L. Stine likes to play pinball on his very own pinball machine and explore New York City with his wife, Jane, and son, Matt.

WIN A TRIP TO MEET
R·L·STINE
...IF YOU DARE!
You could win an exciting weekend in New York City and have lunch with R.L. Stine

1 GRAND PRIZE: A WEEKEND (3 DAY/2 NIGHT) TRIP TO NEW YORK CITY TO MEET R.L. STINE

10 First Prizes: Walkman and an autographed "Ghosts of Fear Street" Audiobook

20 Second Prizes: Autographed "Ghosts of Fear Street" T-Shirt

30 Third Prizes: Autographed "Ghosts of Fear Street" Audiobook

50 Fourth Prizes: Autographed "Ghosts of Fear Street" Book

100 Fifth Prizes: "Ghosts of Fear Street" Sticker

Complete the official entry form and send to:
Pocket Books, GOFS Sweepstakes
1230 Avenue of the Americas, New York, NY 10020

Name_____(Child)

Birthdate_____/_____/_____

Name_____(Parent)

Address _____

City_____State_____Zip_____

Phone (_____)_____

See back for official rules   1302 (1 of 2)

POCKET BOOKS/"GOFS AUDIO" SWEEPSTAKES
Sweepstakes Official Rules:

1. No Purchase Necessary. Enter by mailing the completed Official Entry Form (no copies allowed) or by mailing a 3" x 5" card with your name and address to the Pocket Books/GOFS Sweepstakes,13th Floor, 1230 Avenue of the Americas, NY, NY 10020. Entries must be received by 6/30/97. Not responsible for lost, late, stolen, illegible, mutilated, incomplete, postage due or misdirected entries or mail or for typographical errors in the entry form or rules. Enter as often as you wish, but one entry per envelope. Winners will be selected at random from all eligible entries received in a drawing to be held on or about 7/1/97.

2. Prizes: One Grand Prize: A weekend (three day/two night) trip for up to four persons (the winning minor, one parent or legal guardian and two guests) including round-trip coach airfare from the major U.S. airport nearest the winner's residence to New York City, ground transportation or car rental in New York City, meals, two nights in a hotel (one room, occupancy for four) and lunch with R.L. Stine (approx. retail value $3500.000, trip must be taken on the date specified by Simon & Schuster, Inc.), Ten First Prizes: Walkman and Autographed "Ghosts of Fear Street" Audiobook (approx. retail value $40.00) Twenty Second Prizes: Autographed "Ghosts of Fear Street" T-shirt (approx. retail value $20.00 each), Thirty Third Prizes: Autographed "Ghosts of Fear Street" Audiobook (approx. retail value $7.95 each), Fifty Fourth Prizes: Autographed "Ghosts of Fear Street" Book (approx. retail value: $3.99) One Hundred Fifth Prizes: "Ghosts of Fear Street" Sticker (approx. retail value: $1.00)

3. The sweepstakes is open to residents of the U.S. and Canada, excluding Quebec, not older than fourteen as of 6/30/97. Proof of age required to claim prize. Prizes will be awarded to the winner's parent or legal guardian. Void in Puerto Rico and wherever prohibited or restricted by law. Simon & Schuster, Inc., Parachute Press, Inc., their respecitve officers, directors, shareholders, employees, suppliers, parents, subsidiaries, affiliates, agencies, sponsors, participating retailers, and persons connected with the use, marketing or conduct of this sweepstakes and their families living in the same household, are not eligible.

4. One prize per person or household. Prizes are not transferable and may not be substituted except by sponsor, in event of unavailability, in which case a prize of equal or greater value will be awarded. All prizes will be awarded. The odds of winning a prize depend upon the number of eligible entries received.

5. If a winner is a Canadian resident, then he/she must correctly answer a skill-based question administered by mail.

6. All expenses on receipt and use of prize including Federal, state and local taxes are the sole responsibility of the winners. Winners will be notified by mail. Winners may be required to execute and return an Affidavit of Eligibility and Release and all other legal documents which the sweepstakes sponsor may require (including a W-9 tax form) within 15 days of receipt of notification or an alternate winner will be selected.

7. Winners irrevocably grant Pocket Books, Parachute Press, Inc. and Simon & Schuster Audio the worldwide right, for no additional consideration, to use their names, photographs, likenesses, and entries for any advertising, promotion, marketing and publicity purposes relating to this promotional contest or otherwise without further compensation to or permission from the entrants, except where prohibited by law.

8. Winners agree that Simon & Schuster Inc., Parachute Press, Inc., their respective officers, directors, shareholders, employees, suppliers, parents, subsidiaries, affiliates, agencies, sponsors, participating retailers, and persons connected with the use, marketing or conduct of this sweepstakes, shall have no liability in connection with the collection, acceptance or use of the prizes awarded herein.

9. By participating in this sweepstakes, entrants agree to be bound by these rules and the decisions of the judges and sweepstakes sponsors, which are final in all matters relating to the sweepstakes.

10. For a list of major prize winners, (available after 7/11/97) send a stamped, self-addressed envelope to Prize Winners, Pocket Books/GOFS Sweepstakes, 13th Floor, 1230 Avenue of the Americas, NY, NY 10020.

Is The Roller Coaster Really Haunted?

THE BEAST

❏ 88055-1/$3.99

It Was An Awsome Ride—Through Time!

THE BEAST 2

❏ 52951-X/$3.99

A MINSTREL®BOOK

Published by Pocket Books

Simon & Schuster Mail Order Dept. BWB
200 Old Tappan Rd., Old Tappan, N.J. 07675
Please send me the books I have checked above. I am enclosing $_____(please add $0.75 to cover the postage and handling for each order. Please add appropriate sales tax). Send check or money order--no cash or C.O.D.'s please. Allow up to six weeks for delivery. For purchase over $10.00 you may use VISA: card number, expiration date and customer signature must be included.

Name _____
Address _____
City _____ State/Zip _____
VISA Card # _____ Exp.Date _____
Signature _____ 1163